Oyster Moon

For Jaimie,
With Best Wishes,

Margaret Meacham

Oyster Moon

BY MARGARET MEACHAM

Illustrated by Marcy Dunn Ramsey

TIDEWATER PUBLISHERS
Centreville, Maryland

Library of Congress Cataloging-in-Publication Data

Meacham, Margaret
    Oyster moon / by Margaret Meacham ; illustrated by Marcy Dunn Ramsey. — 1st ed.
        p.   cm
        Summary: Set in 1885 on Maryland's eastern shore of the Chesapeake Bay, a fourteen-year-old girl rescues her twin brother from the clutches of the cruel captain of an oyster dredge during the height of the Oyster Wars.
    ISBN 0-87033-459-X (paper)
    [1. Oysters—Fiction. 2. Chesapeake Bay Region (Md. and Va.) — Fiction. 3. Maryland—Fiction. 4. Twins—Fiction. 5. Brothers and sisters—Fiction.]   I. Ramsey, Marcy Dunn, ill. II. Title.
    PZ7.M478860y 1996
    [Fic]—dc20   96-15057

Manufactured in the United States of America
First edition

For Katy

Acknowledgments

I am indebted to Dr. John Wennersten of Salisbury, Maryland, for his book, *The Oyster Wars of Chesapeake Bay*, and for his helpful comments on my manuscript. It was his book, and the story of the German immigrant Otto Mayher who died on the oyster boat *Eva* in 1884, that inspired *Oyster Moon*.

For their help with the research for this book, and for generously sharing their own stories, my sincere thanks to the following people: Ms. Olga Crouch of Turkey Point, Maryland; Captain Elmer Riggins of Crisfield, Maryland; Mr. Lawrence W. Burgess of the Eastern Shore Early Americana Museum and Country Store in Marion, Maryland; Ms. Scotti Oliver, curator of the Maryland Room of the Talbot County Library; Ms. Jackie Brooks and Mr. Don Brooks of Crisfield, Maryland; and the staffs of the Maryland Historical Association in Baltimore; the Chesapeake Bay Maritime Museum in St. Michaels, Maryland; and the Mt. Zion One-Room School in Snow Hill, Maryland.

Finally, my deepest thanks to my friend James Williams for all the Eastern Shore stories he has given me over the years. To me, a story is the greatest gift. I hope you like this one.

One

Before the first light, when the air was cold and damp and the river outside was black, Anna woke up. She lay under her quilts, warm and still, listening. She heard her father downstairs, arranging the hot coals in the woodstove with the poker. She heard his footsteps crossing the kitchen, and Willy scratching on the back door to be let out.

"Hush now, mutt," she heard her father murmur as he and Willy went out to the woodpile. She heard her mother's softer footsteps, the rattling of pots, the clink of utensils.

A golden shaft of light from the oil lamp in the kitchen crept upstairs to the loft, and Anna could see Margaret's small sleeping face on the pillow beside her. Across the loft, Noah lay in his bed, a motionless lump in a tangle of blankets. And beside Noah was the empty, silent space where Toby should have been.

Soon Anna would smell coffee and corn pone and then, just as a pale streak of purple dawn was breaking over the Bay, her father would leave the cottage and head for the Bay to begin his day's work. It was cold, wet, muscle-aching work, but Anna knew that tonging for oysters was her father's life, the only life he could imagine.

Usually, when Anna happened to wake up this early, she would roll over and sink even deeper beneath the covers, knowing she still had an hour before she had to be up. But this morning she couldn't go back to sleep.

It had happened again—another message. This was the third one. Three times now, three mornings in a row. This morning, still half asleep, Anna had felt under her pillow for the scrap of paper. She had known it would be there, had known she would find it, just like the other two.

"Otto is dead," the first message said.

"They killed him," the second one said.

"Help," said the third. She could barely read it in the dawn light.

The messages were written on scraps of paper torn from her journal. They were written in her own handwriting, so she must have written them herself, but she had no memory of doing it. She had no idea who Otto was, or who "they" were.

Anna knew that some people walked and talked in their sleep, but writing? She had never heard of anyone writing anything when they were sound asleep.

Anyway, it really didn't matter whether she had written the messages herself. She knew that Toby had sent them.

Later, as she sat on the beach watching her five-year-old sister Margaret and her seven-year-old brother Noah, Anna pulled the three scraps out of her apron pocket and studied them once again. She had looked at them so often that the handwritten letters no longer seemed to form recognizable words. They had taken on a new meaning, like a word you repeat again and again until it finally loses its meaning and becomes something else.

A few feet away, Margaret dug in the sand, a pile of shells and stones beside her.

"Are you going to keep all of those, Margaret?" Anna asked.

Margaret nodded. "Look at this one." She held up a smooth pink shell.

"It's pretty," Anna said. "Why don't you just keep that one and leave the rest?"

But Margaret shook her head. She looked over at Anna and noticed the scraps of paper in her hand. "What are those, Anna?" Margaret asked.

"Nothing," Anna said, putting them back into the pocket of her apron.

Margaret frowned. "They're *something*. I saw them. If they were nothing I couldn't see them," she said.

"They're nothing you need to know about," Anna said.

"Why won't you ever tell me anything?" Margaret whined.

"Just forget about it, Margaret. There's nothing to tell," Anna snapped.

Margaret began lining her shells up on the sand in front of her. After a few minutes she said, "Noah's loony. And he's chased all the sea gulls away."

Noah stood on the outermost rock of the breakwater. He was singing, shouting the words out into the wind as loud as he could.

"Who does he think he is? Miss Ruth Tibbits?" Margaret snickered.

Miss Ruth Tibbits had the loudest voice in the church choir. Every Sunday she bellowed out the hymns, her words flying up to the ceiling, swirling around the rafters, and roaring back down to wake even the sleepiest of the congregation.

Out on the rock Noah sang, "Aunt Phoebe tells fibs, Aunt Phoebe tells fibs. She is a fibber, a fibber she is." He sang it again and again, puffing out his chest and marching in place.

"Noah! That's enough," Anna called. "Come on in before you get soaked." The tide was coming in and the wake from a steamboat threw up a spray.

He turned to look at them, glanced down at the water, and took a giant step onto the next rock in.

"Well, she does, you know," he said.

"Who does what?" Anna asked.

"Aunt Phoebe tells fibs. Isn't that right, Margaret."

Margaret nodded solemnly, looking from Anna to Noah.

"What are you going on about?" Anna asked him.

"Aunt Phoe-be. When she was here on Sunday she was watching Pa in the dory and she said, 'I declare,' " Noah put his hands on his hips and spoke in a high falsetto voice, " 'I believe your father has Bay water in his veins instead of blood.' " He took his hands off his hips and went on in his regular voice. "And that's a fib. He'd be dead if it were true."

"It's just a manner of speaking," Anna told him. "She means that Pa loves the water."

"Well, I still think she's foolish. Remember when she screamed just 'cause the chicken flew at her? Whoever heard of a growed woman that's scared of a little bitty chicken?" Noah laughed, remembering how Aunt Phoebe had yelled last Sunday when the chicken came at her. Anna smiled too. It had been a sight.

Noah saw that he had made Anna smile, and he raced around on the beach, flapping his arms and shrieking, "It's a chicken. A big, bad chicken. Help! Help!"

"Noah! My shells. Watch out for my shells," Margaret screamed.

As she helped Margaret collect her stones and shells Anna said, "Aunt Phoebe doesn't keep chickens up in Baltimore. She's just not used to them, is all."

Noah stopped running and flopped down onto the sand. "Seems to me they don't have much up there. Aunt Phoebe doesn't have chickens. She doesn't have a boat. What does she have?" he asked.

"Baltimore is a city. They have city things. Aunt Phoebe's used to city ways," Anna explained.

"And we're used to the water. I'm glad we live on Heron Point, aren't you, Anna?" Noah asked.

Anna gazed out across the Bay. It was a calico day; at least, that's what she called days like this. Clear and shiny, the bright blue water was dotted with the white sails of the oyster drudgers, like a huge piece of the blue calico material that Mama made their dresses from. "Drudgers" was what the people around here called the boats that dredged oysters from the Bay. Closer to shore, near the mouth of the river, tongers bobbed on the shoals in their smaller boats, pulling up oysters with tongs from the bottom of the Chesapeake.

11

Once Anna had thought she would never grow tired of that sight. She was like her pa that way. She loved the Bay. She loved the water. Not just for oystering and crabbing, but for swimming too. Ever since she was a tiny little girl, younger than Margaret, she had loved the water. And she could outswim any boy or girl in Heron's Harbor. Every now and then some boy would take it into his head that he could beat her, and would challenge her to a swimming race, but Anna always won. Even Toby admitted she was the fastest swimmer around.

But lately, when Anna looked out across the Bay she no longer saw the miles and miles of blue water. Instead she saw the throbbing greens of a jungle, the cold, majestic purple of a mountain range, the jumbling, swirling colors of a city, and she felt a restlessness that even the lapping of the waves and the rhythm of the tides couldn't dispel.

"Well? Aren't you?" Noah demanded.

"Aren't I what?" Anna asked.

"Glad we live here?"

"Yes. Of course I am," Anna assured him, because the things she was feeling were far too complicated to explain to a seven-year-old.

The sun was getting lower in the west now, and Anna knew it would soon be time to take Noah and Margaret back up to the house. She hoped that later she would have time to sneak down to the old lighthouse. Maybe there she could find some peace and quiet, some time to puzzle out what to do about the mysterious messages.

Although they weren't really such a mystery. They were from Toby, of course.

Toby was Anna's twin brother. Anna had been born ninety seconds before Toby, so, technically, she was older. She was also bigger, outweighing Toby by almost half a pound at birth. And she had stayed bigger than him until just about six months ago when he had started to shoot up. Now he was taller than her by almost three inches.

Anna didn't know if all twins were like Toby and herself, able to communicate in ways that didn't involve speaking. Sometimes it was almost as if they shared one mind. Her mother had told her that when they were babies, they would start to cry at exactly the same moment, even if they were in separate rooms. And they had never been able to play Hide and Seek or Prisoner's Base because they were able to go right to each other's hiding spot without even thinking about it. Once Anna had tried hiding in the bushes and imagining that she was in the outhouse. When Toby found her he had said, "You almost hid in the outhouse, didn't you?"

But now Toby was gone and Anna felt like part of her insides was gone too, like there was a hole right down inside of her. He had left almost two weeks ago, shipped out on an oyster drudge boat. In the first few days after he had gone Anna had tried and tried to get a picture, or a feeling—something, anything—from him, but there had been nothing. It was odd. She had never felt this nothingness before. She wondered if this was how other people, people who didn't have a twin, felt. Maybe it wouldn't have been so bad if she hadn't been used to having him there, in some corner of her mind almost all the time.

Anna knew that her mother missed him too, though she tried to hide it. Like last night. Anna and her mother had been sitting at the long wooden table peeling vegetables for the stew. Noah was squirming around on the floor, and Ma had said, "Noah, for heaven's sake. God gave you legs so you could stand on them. Why on earth are you wiggling all over the floor?"

"I'm a water snake, Mama. I can't walk. I can only swim," he said, squirming his way across the room.

Margaret lay down on the floor beside him. "I'm a water snake, too," she said, trying to squirm like Noah.

"No," Noah told her. "You can't be a water snake. You have to be something else."

"Then I'll be an oyster," Margaret said, curling up in a ball. "And Toby will catch me and I'll get to see him."

Noah stopped squirming and sat up. "When is Toby coming home, Mama?" he asked.

"I can't say exactly, Noah. Whenever the boat he's on comes in."

"Will he be home before Christmas?"

"I expect so. I'm sure the men want to be with their families at Christmas."

"But the drudgers are bad. Pa said so. Maybe they don't care about their families."

"Hush, now, Noah," Mama said, which was what she always said when she couldn't think of an answer. And then her eyes got wet and she put down the carrot she was peeling and picked up an onion.

"These onions do make my eyes water," she said, taking out her handkerchief. But Anna knew her eyes had been wet before she started peeling the onion. And carrots didn't make anyone's eyes water.

Pa wouldn't talk about Toby, but Anna knew he was as mad as a blue crab in a net. He hated the oyster drudgers almost as much as he hated the politicians from Annapolis and the city slickers from Baltimore who were always trying to control the watermen, always making up new laws and new taxes.

Her father was a tonger, catching oysters the way they were supposed to be caught, he said, not like the drudgers who were ruining the oyster beds and stealing what was rightfully his. Besides, he claimed, the drudgers were god-less, ruthless men who would do anything for money.

Sitting on the beach, Anna wondered if he hated Toby now that Toby had disobeyed him and gone off with a drudger.

Was Toby on one of those boats way out there on the Bay? Why had he sent her the messages? Was he in trouble? Her hand was on its way to her pocket to touch the scraps again when Noah jumped up and pointed to a small gray cloud on the horizon. "There she comes. There comes the steamer," he cried, racing down the beach. "Hurry up. We've got to get to town. She'll be at the docks in half an hour."

Noah had dreams of being a steamboat captain someday, and he never missed a chance to see one come in.

Today, Anna wanted to see it dock too, not because she had any particular interest in steamboats, but because today was the day their new teacher was due to arrive from Balti-more, and Anna couldn't wait to get a look at her. Anna and Margaret gathered up their stones and shells and followed Noah up the path to the house.

In the yard, Ma was hanging out the laundry. When Noah

saw her he shouted, "She's coming, Mama. Can we go to meet her?"

Ma spoke around the clothespins sticking out of her mouth. "Go on, but be back in time for supper." She turned to look at them and, taking the pins out of her mouth, added, "And stay out of trouble. You'll go too, won't you, Anna?"

Anna shrugged. "Might as well, I guess." She tried to sound uninterested, but her mother wasn't fooled.

Ma narrowed her eyes and peered closely at Anna. "Now don't you go letting your curiosity run away with you. The poor woman's had a long trip. She'll want to get to her rooms and get settled. Don't you go giving her any chitchat. You'll meet her tomorrow along with all the other children."

All the other children, Anna thought. As if she was one of them. Her mother made her so angry when she said things like that, acting as if she wasn't any older than Noah. And here she was, fourteen years old, the oldest student in the school, and helper to Mrs. Phibbs for the past two years, ever since Toby had quit school to start oystering with Pa. After Mrs. Phibbs took sick back in September Anna had practically taught the children all by herself. Then Mrs. Phibbs had gotten worse, and for the last three weeks there hadn't been any school. Now they were finally getting a new teacher. Anna couldn't wait to see what she would be like.

"Oh, wait. Since you're going to town you might as well be useful. Take a dozen eggs to Mr. Crick, and ask him to fill the molasses jar, would you, Anna?" her mother said. "I do believe we're clean out."

"Can we have a penny for some candy, Mama? Please?" Noah begged.

"There's none to spare, child. You know that as well as I do," Ma said with a sigh. "And not likely to be anytime soon, oystering being what it is this year."

"When Toby gets back, he'll have lots of money. Then we can buy cartloads of candy," Noah said.

"Hmmm. We'll see about that," Ma said, turning back to the clothesline. She took one of Pa's shirts out of the basket and pinned it to the line. "Don't forget to take the molasses jar, Anna."

"Come on, Margaret. Hurry up, Anna," Noah shouted from the road where he was hopping with impatience, his bare feet kicking up clouds of dust.

"Noah, you get in the house and put your shoes and stockings on. It's getting too cold to go to town barefoot. It's the middle of October," Ma called.

"Aw, Ma, it's as warm as July. And we'll miss the docking if we don't go quick."

"Noah Shipherd, don't give me your back talk. You get inside this instant and put on your shoes."

Noah stomped into the house, his face stormy, as Anna went to the kitchen to get the molasses jar. Finally, they set off for town. As they walked, Anna fingered the scraps of paper in her pocket once again. Knowing they were there made her feel all kinds of things. Glad, and mad, and scared, all at the same time.

Part of her was glad to have Toby back again in that corner of her mind. But she was mad too. It was so like him, getting himself in trouble and leaving it to her to bail him out.

And part of her was just plain scared.

Otto is dead. They killed him. Help.

Fine, she thought. But just what exactly was she supposed to do?

Two

Finally they would see their new teacher, Anna thought, as she followed Noah and Margaret down the road. Her name was Miss Winslow, but that was all Anna knew about her.

Anna had been thinking about Miss Winslow for weeks, ever since she first heard that she was coming to replace Mrs. Phibbs. She had been wondering what she would look like, and if she had been educated in Baltimore. Maybe at one of the schools Aunt Phoebe was always talking about.

Aunt Phoebe wanted Anna to come to Baltimore and go to what she called a proper school. As if their school wasn't a proper school. But Anna's father was dead set against it. He didn't hold with too much book learning, especially for girls, Anna had heard him tell Ma. She remembered how Ma's lips had tightened as she looked down at her sewing when he said that, and Pa had said quickly, "Well, seems to me the school here is just fine."

"But she'll soon outgrow it," her mother had said. "And she does have a quick mind," she added.

Her father had glanced at Anna, who tried to look as if she hadn't been listening. "And she'll soon have a swollen head as well," he had said.

That had been the end of the conversation, but it had been just the beginning of Anna's thinking on the subject. It seemed to pop into her mind all the time now. Did she want to go, or didn't she? Anna didn't know quite how she felt about it. One minute she couldn't think of anything more exciting than going to school in Baltimore, and the next minute she couldn't imagine ever leaving Heron's Harbor.

Perhaps the new teacher could help her decide, Anna thought.

Anna waved to Nellie, who was waiting with her brother Thomas at the usual spot, under the big oak tree on the town road.

"Hurry up," Thomas yelled. "It's almost in." The two boys and Margaret raced on ahead, but Nellie waited until Anna caught up to her and then took her arm.

The minute Nellie grabbed her arm Anna knew she had something to tell her. Nellie's face was flushed, and her eyes were shining with importance.

"Mother's already gone ahead in the cart, but I waited for you," Nellie said. "You'll never guess what's happened," she said in her imitation grown-up voice.

"What's happened, Nellie?" Anna asked.

"She's not coming."

"Who's not coming?"

"Miss Winslow, of course. Who else would I be talking about?"

Miss Winslow was going to be staying with the Perrys in

their extra room. Since Mr. Perry had died two years back, the Perrys often took in paying guests to help with expenses.

"What do you mean she's not coming?" Anna demanded. "That's impossible. She has to come."

"Well, she's not. Mother's had a telegram. Her father took sick and she can't leave him. They're sending someone else in her place."

"Someone else?" Anna cried. "Well, who? What's her name?"

Nellie didn't say anything for a minute. Anna knew she was relishing the suspense. "It's not a she," she said finally.

Anna stopped and stared at Nellie. "Not a she? You mean—"

Nellie nodded. "A man."

"A man," Anna repeated. "But we've never had a man for a teacher. What's he like? How old is he?"

"I don't know anything about him. Except his name."

"Well, tell me. What is it?" Anna was getting exasperated. Nellie was always like this, making Anna pull every detail out of her, keeping her in suspense as long as she could whenever she knew something Anna didn't. That happened a lot because the Perrys lived closer to town, and Mrs. Perry loved to gossip.

Nellie flung her braid over her shoulder. "His name," she paused, glancing at Anna, "is Mr. Grim. Mr. Matthew Grim. I think he must be real old, because Mama said he will require peace and quiet in the evenings and that Thomas and I mustn't carry on."

Anna's heart sank. She had pictured their new teacher as a kind young woman who would give her private instruction and who would depend upon her for help with the younger children.

"Mr. Grim . . ." she said.

"Mr. Matthew Grim," Nellie repeated.

"I wonder what he looks like," Anna said.

"I think he'll be horrid-looking," Nellie said matter-of-factly. "He'll probably have a big red nose and blotchy skin, and hair growing out of his ears."

"And a potbelly and spindly little legs like sticks," Anna added.

"A hunchback, and false teeth that clatter when he talks," Nellie laughed.

"A wart with hair sticking out of it on his chin."

"And he'll smell like mothballs."

By the time they got to the steamer dock Mr. Grim had become monstrous.

They were just in time to see the steamboat come chugging 'round the bend. Her whistle sounded, and a ripple of excitement swept through the crowd waiting on the dock.

The landing was alive with noise and color. People were shouting and waving, animals were braying, and the roustabouts were chanting and singing as they hauled the sacks of wheat and potatoes, bushels of oysters, barrels of fish and crabs that would be loaded on the steamer for the return trip to Baltimore.

The steamboat slowed as it came towards the dock, the sidewheel reversed with a big wash of water, and the boat nudged itself into the dock. The stevedores lowered the gangplank, and the few passengers who were getting off at Heron's Harbor came straggling down to the wharf.

Anna and Nellie knew who most of them were. There was Freddie Harrison's Aunt Philona, who was visiting from Baltimore. There was Mr. Thompson, who owned the big farm on the other side of town, and there was Mr. Blackburn, who owned Blackburn's Oysters, a shucking and packing plant in Heron's Harbor.

Then there was Mrs. Constable, who had been up to Baltimore for shopping and was laden down with boxes and parcels. She was all dressed up in her Sunday finest, but her dress was all wrinkly and her hat askew, and she looked hot and tired from her journey. As she wrestled with her parcels, a man in city clothes stepped up next to her and spoke. Anna guessed that he was offering to help her, for she smiled and handed him a large box. Then, carrying his own suitcase in his other hand, he followed Mrs. Constable down the gangplank.

When he reached the wharf he handed Mrs. Constable her box, set down his own case, and looked around as if he wasn't quite sure where to go. He took out a handkerchief and wiped his face, and stood there looking hot and tired and somehow out of place, like a mallard duck in a flock of geese.

Nellie nudged Anna. "Do you think that's him?"

"I don't know. He doesn't look at all like what we thought."

"He's so handsome," Nellie whispered excitedly. "I just love that kind of mustache. And his clothes—all the latest!" Nellie liked to think she knew all about what was fashionable in Baltimore.

When Mrs. Perry hurried over to the man, Anna and Nellie knew for certain that it was Mr. Grim.

Nellie's hand tightened on Anna's arm. "It's him. It *is* him," she whispered. "And he'll be living in my house! Can you imagine?"

Mrs. Perry was leading Mr. Grim down the wharf towards the cart. When she caught sight of Nellie and Anna she waved them over.

"Well, Mr. Grim, here are two of your pupils right here," Mrs. Perry exclaimed. She put her hand on Nellie's shoulder and gave her a little shove toward Mr. Grim. "This is my Nellie." Nellie curtseyed and said, "Pleased to make your acquaintance, sir."

"And this is Anna Shipherd," Mrs. Perry nodded at Anna, "our neighbor from down the point. I think you'll find them both fine pupils."

Mr. Grim smiled as he shook their hands. "Excellent. I was hoping I would have some older students. Can I count on you ladies to help me with the young ones? My experience so far has been with high school students, so I'll need all the help I can get."

"Yes, sir. Oh, yes, sir. We were Mrs. Phibbs's assistants, weren't we, Anna?" Nellie gave her an elbow in the ribs that nearly knocked her over.

Anna nodded. Mr. Grim turned to her, smiling warmly, and as she looked into his brown eyes, Anna felt her knees begin to quiver. She could barely trust her voice to answer.

"We'll be pleased to help out, sir," she managed to stammer.

"Well, we'd best get on home and show you to your room, Mr. Grim. I'm sure you must be tired after your journey," Mrs. Perry said, leading Mr. Grim to her cart. He threw his suitcase in and climbed up onto the passenger's seat. Nellie hopped in the back. "Aren't you coming?" she asked Anna.

"I have an errand to do for Mama," she told them.

As the cart rattled up the road towards the Perrys', Anna looked around for Noah and Margaret and spotted them on the other side of the wharf talking to some of the other children.

She crossed the wharf and called them to come with her to Crick's.

The store was busy, as it usually was on steamboat days. Mr. Crick was cutting plugs of tobacco for Captain Ewell, and Mrs. Crick was hovering near the bolts of drygoods trying to help Mrs. Barker make her selection. When Mrs. Barker saw Anna she cried, "Anna Shipherd, I declare, the Lord must have sent you to me. Step over here just a minute, if you don't mind, darlin'."

Anna went over to Mrs. Barker, who pulled several yards of pink cloth from the bolt and held it up to her.

"You don't mind, do you, dear? I'm trying to choose some fabric to make a new dress for Carrie and I can't seem to make up my mind. Your coloring is just like hers."

"That one looks lovely," said Mrs. Crick.

Anna stood patiently while the two women draped her with various fabrics as if she were a mannequin. Finally Mrs. Barker made her choice, and Mrs. Crick cut it for her.

"Mama sent these eggs and asked can we fill the molasses jar?" Anna told Mrs. Crick.

"Go right ahead, dear," Mrs. Crick told her, taking the eggs. "And I believe I have some mail for you. Let me get it."

Anna filled the jar with molasses from the big barrel. When she was finished Mrs. Crick was back with their mail.

There was her mother's copy of *Home Monthly*, a letter

from Aunt Phoebe, something for her father from the bank, and . . . wait, what was this, she wondered. It was an envelope that was scuffed and folded, with her name and address written in a rough, hurried hand. But some of the letters looked familiar. Toby, she thought as she studied the address. Yes, she was almost certain it was Toby's handwriting!

At last, she thought as she tore open the envelope, at last some news of Toby. But when she took the letter out, she saw that it was not from Toby. Not only was it written in a hand she had never seen before, it was in a language she couldn't read. She couldn't make out one word of the letter.

What on earth, Anna thought. She turned over the envelope and studied the handwriting. She was almost certain that the address, at least, had been written by Toby. But why? Why would he send her a letter written in a foreign language? What was she supposed to do with it? And what did it mean?

She looked the letter over again. She still couldn't read any of it, but at the bottom of the page this time she noticed the signature of the letter writer. And there she saw the only word she recognized: Otto. The letter was signed by someone named Otto Ferdinand Grüner.

Three

"There he is again. The man Noah and I were talking to down at the wharf," Margaret said.

Anna glanced at the man Margaret was pointing to. She'd never seen him before, but she had the feeling he had been watching them just now. In fact, she was sure of it. But when she faced him, he turned his head away and pretended to be examining the knives in the case on the far counter.

As they went out the door Anna turned back once more to look at the man. He stared at them dully, his red-veined, lifeless eyes partially obscured by dirty, matted hair. His gray skin was pockmarked and streaked with grime. As they left, Anna noticed that one of his hands was purple and swollen, more than twice the size it should have been. Oyster hand. Anna had seen it many times before. If an oysterman cut his hand on an oyster and didn't treat it right away, the cut would become infected, and the hand would swell up horribly.

Anna shivered. She didn't like the way he seemed to be watching them.

As they left the store Margaret whispered, "I didn't like that man."

"Me either," Anna said.

It was getting to be dusk. A bank of clouds covered the sun, and the sky turned gray. Overhead, three black turkey vultures circled, watching the earth below for prey. As they walked towards home, one of the birds swooped down and landed in the ditch by the roadside. It was over two feet tall, and looked as if it weighed almost as much as Margaret. Noah scooped a handful of dirt and threw it, and the bird spread its wings but it didn't fly off. It glared at them, its hooded eyes staring unblinkingly as they passed, as if daring them to try to take its prey. Something about the bird reminded Anna of the man in the store and she took Margaret's hand and hurried her up the road.

At home, Mama was making apple butter and the house smelled sweetly of autumn.

"Anna, is that you?" Mama called.

"Yes, Mama. It's us."

"Did you get the molasses?"

"Yes, Mama. And the mail," Anna told her, putting the molasses on the kitchen shelf and the mail, except for the strange letter addressed to her, on the table. Her mother was stirring the apple pulp in the big pot. She glanced at Anna. "Well, did you see her?"

Anna smiled, realizing that her mother was almost as curious about the teacher as she herself had been. Now she knew how Nellie felt when she had news to tell.

"I didn't see *her*, but I did see our new teacher," Anna teased.

Her mother's brow wrinkled. "What kind of an answer is that?"

"Just what it sounds like," Anna said.

"I don't have time for riddles, missy. Did you see the new teacher or not?"

Anna couldn't keep it in any longer. "Mama, it's a man!"

Her mother's wooden spoon froze in midair. "A man? But I thought it was to be a Miss Winslow."

Anna explained about Miss Winslow's father and the telegram. "His name is Mr. Grim. Nellie and I thought he'd be horrid-looking, but . . ."

"But what?"

"Well, he's actually kind of nice-looking."

"A man. Well, I'll be," her mother said, shaking her head.

Anna helped her mother ladle the apple butter into crocks. The letter in her pocket was burning like a hot ash. Should she tell Mama about it? Why had Toby sent it to her? If he had wanted their parents to know, wouldn't he have sent it to them?

"You look tired, Anna. Is something troubling you? Are you worried about this new teacher?"

"No, it's not that, Mama . . ."

She didn't want to look into her mother's eyes for fear she would be sucked right into them, and would forget that she couldn't tell her what was on her mind.

Her mother's eyes were like that. A deep blue, like the Bay, and like the Bay, you could dive right in and forget all about yourself. She had loved that when she was a little girl, but now that she was older, she didn't always want to dive in. She didn't want to lose herself. There were things about her that her mother couldn't understand, things she knew that she couldn't tell her. She couldn't tell her about the letter. She knew that Toby wouldn't want her to. She would have to watch what she said.

"It's nothing, Mama. I'm just tired, is all."

"Well, I hope this man knows what he's doing. He'll have his hands full. Noah and Thomas Perry are like wild animals. They've gotten away with murder these last few weeks with Mrs. Phibbs being indisposed."

"Oh, Mama, he'll be fine. And anyway, Noah and Thomas aren't half as bad as Billy Pittman or Jake Mason." Anna put the tops on the crocks and wiped them off. "He wants Nellie and me to be his assistants," she went on.

Her mother sniffed and closed her mouth tight in the way she had when she didn't want to say what she was thinking. Anna saw her mother's Adam's apple moving as if the words were stacked up in her throat trying to get out.

"You don't think we're old enough, do you?" Anna asked her.

"I think you need some more learning before you try to teach others," her mother admitted.

Anna nodded. "Do you think I should go live with Aunt Phoebe and go to school in Baltimore?" she asked.

"We'll see. We'll see."

"Mama, don't you ever miss Baltimore? I mean, you did grow up there . . ."

Anna's mother was a Baltimore girl who had met her father when her choral group came to sing in the Heron's

Harbor Church. Anna remembered what her mother had told her about the potluck supper the church had put on after the concert. "Your father just plopped himself right down beside me at that dinner, and didn't leave my side all night," her mother had told Anna with a mixture of pride and amusement in her voice. Her eyes had gotten a dreamy, faraway look as she remembered that long ago spring night.

And then, that summer, Anna's father had worked on a buy boat bringing crabs up to the Baltimore harbor. And every time he came to town he would call on her mother. "He was so different from the Baltimore boys I knew. He seemed so strong and so sure of himself in a quiet sort of way," her mother had told her.

Now her mother put the crocks of apple butter up on the shelf. "I missed Baltimore something awful when we first moved over here. I was so lonely. And I thought the people over here were savages. Why, they didn't have fine houses, or fancy shops, and the church was a tiny little wooden shack. I thought I'd come to the end of the earth."

"What did you do?" Anna asked.

Her mother smiled. "I got used to it."

"That's all?" Anna asked. "You just got used to it?"

"Well, eventually I grew to love it, but that took a while. At first I used to spend my time thinking about how I could get back to Baltimore. I actually believed I might be able to talk your father into leaving Heron's Harbor and moving up there." Her mother smiled and shook her head. "But after a while I realized that asking your father to move to Baltimore would be like asking a rockfish to leave the water and live on the land. It just wouldn't work. That's when I figured out that I had better learn to like it here."

"So how did you do that?" Anna asked.

"Well, the first thing I did was make a friend. After that, the rest was easy."

Anna nodded. She had never thought about her mother as a lonely young woman. It was hard to imagine.

"Was Mrs. Perry your first friend here, Mama?"

"Goodness, no. I didn't meet Mrs. Perry until after Nellie was born. You and Toby were almost two years old by then. No, my first friend was a woman named Mrs. Lantree. She was a member of the women's guild at the church, and she invited me to come help embroider the altar cloth. I've never been so grateful to anyone in my life."

"What happened to Mrs. Lantree?"

"She died, oh, it must be ten years ago now. But the Lord knows I'll never forget her. She was a good soul."

Through the window Anna watched Noah and Margaret as they played in the yard. The sky was growing darker and the wind off the Bay sent little miniature tornadoes of sand and dust swirling around the clothes on the line.

Ma was scrubbing out the pot. Anna watched her as she worked. She watched her hands as they moved over the surface of the pot. Anna loved her mother's hands. How many times they had brushed and braided Anna's hair, felt her forehead for fever, tied her apron, and tugged her collar into place. Anna could do all those things herself now, of course, but still she loved the gentle touch of those strong hands.

Anna wanted to tell her mother about Toby, about how she thought he was in trouble. But she knew she couldn't tell anyone about the letter. He had sent it to her alone. She knew she should keep it to herself, but she had to say something.

"Mama?"

"Yes, Anna?"

"I'm worried about Toby. I've been getting feelings that . . . that he's in trouble."

Her mother's hands stopped moving, and when she turned to look at Anna, Anna saw fear blow across her face like a cloud across the sun. But it was gone as quickly as it came, and her mother said, "Toby's way out on the Bay, child. Too far away for you to know if he's in trouble or not. You're just missing him, is all."

"Maybe, but I'm still worried," Anna said.

"I worry too, Anna, but worrying doesn't do much good. Nobody but God can help him now, and I have to believe that if he's in trouble, God will find a way to help him. I pray for him every day, and that relieves my worry a bit." Her mother put a hand to Anna's head and smoothed her hair. "You might try it too, Anna."

"Yes, Mama," Anna mumbled.

Four

A shaft of moonlight lit the loft with an eerie silver glow. Something had awakened Anna. Beside her, Margaret slept undisturbed, her soft, even breathing somehow comforting. And across the loft, Noah lay on his pallet, snoring lightly.

Anna sat up, listening, trying not to disturb Margaret. The little girl was a light sleeper, and often woke during the night. Noah, unlike Margaret, tossed and turned and fought sleep, but when it finally overcame him he was out for the night, hardly moving until the next morning when Anna had to shake him until his eyes popped open.

What woke her up? Was it Toby again, sending her messages? She felt under her pillow, but there was nothing. She had not been writing in her sleep this time. But something had awakened her. A noise? A dream? Something.

Anna slipped out of bed and tiptoed across the loft. Downstairs, she could see Willy in his spot in front of the hearth. He was sitting up, looking at the door, his ears pricked as if he too had heard something. Anna crept quietly down the ladder. Willy glanced at her, his tail thumping a few beats when he saw her. Then he stood up, looking toward the door, and Anna heard a low, rumbling growl starting in his throat.

"What is it, boy? Did you hear it, too?" She took hold of the dog's collar and led him to the window, her heart thumping in her chest.

It was a still, silent night, lit by the three-quarters moon that hung over the Bay like a huge white face. At first, Anna saw nothing but their backyard, familiar as always, even in the eerie moonlight. But then she saw him—the same man she had seen at the store that day. He stood in the shadows of the willow trees in one corner of the yard. He was watching the house. Anna felt as if he was looking right at them and she remembered his cold gray eyes and felt their icy stare. Willy saw him and barked, and the man raced across the yard and vanished into the woods beside the house.

Anna let out a small scream, clamping her hand over her mouth to stifle it.

"Anna?" her father called from her parents' bedroom. "Anna? Is that you?"

She heard the floorboards squeaking under his feet as he crossed to the door of the bedroom. Then he was standing in the doorway in his night shirt. "What is it?"

"I heard a noise. I came down, and I saw a man . . . a man out in the yard."

Her father moved to the window to see where Anna was pointing. "He's gone now," she told him. "He heard Willy bark and he ran into the woods." She knelt beside Willy and gave him a hug, rubbing her cheek against the warm, smooth fur on top of his head. "You scared him away, didn't you, boy?"

Her father took his shotgun down from the rack on the wall, stepped into his boots, and went outside to check the shed and the chicken house. Willy ran ahead of him barking, showing off his bravery.

Anna's mother appeared wrapped in a shawl over her flannel nightgown. "What's going on?" she asked. The oil lamp she held in one hand cast flickering shadows across her face.

"There was a man outside by the willows," Anna explained all over again. "He ran when Willy barked, but Pa's gone to check."

"My lands, what next?" her mother asked. "First your brother runs off, and now someone's sneaking around here at night. What on earth for?"

"Probably just someone lost," Anna said. She didn't want to tell them she had seen the same man in town. Something stopped her.

Anna was shivering. It was as much from fear as from cold. Her mother came and put an arm around her. "You'd best get back under the covers, child. You'll catch your death. Pa will make sure everything's all right."

Anna climbed back up to the loft and slipped into bed beside Margaret. She fell asleep quickly, but the man's gray eyes haunted her dreams, and when she woke up the next morning she couldn't get rid of that unsettled feeling.

As Anna dressed for school she thought about the letter. She was positive that Toby had sent it, but what did it mean? What was she supposed to do with it? She went to her chest and checked inside to make sure the envelope was still there where she had hidden it the night before. She felt underneath her clothing and found it, along with the three scraps of paper.

"What's that?" Noah asked.

"It's nothing," Anna said. "Why don't you mind your own business?"

Noah was edging closer to Anna, trying to get a look at the envelope. He was the worst snoop. She knew that, now that he had seen it, he would look for it. She would have to find another place to hide it. She thought of the old lighthouse, the hiding place that she and Toby had devised, a place under the floor that no one could find unless they knew about it. She would go there after school and hide it. And in the meantime, she would think about what to do.

Anna hurried through breakfast. She wanted to get to school early so that she and Nellie could help Mr. Grim set up. Margaret and Noah were dawdling as usual. Noah poured molasses over his corn pone, using way too much. Anna frowned. "Look at that, Mama. He's so wasteful."

"I love molasses. I'll eat every bit," Noah said, taking a big bite and dribbling molasses down his chin.

"You won't. You never do," Anna told him. "And wipe your chin. It's supposed to go in your mouth, not on your face."

"Children, please," said her mother.

"Look at him, Mama. It's disgusting. Eating with him makes me lose my appetite."

Anna drank the last of her glass of milk and took her dishes to the sink. "I promised Nellie I'd meet her early so we can help Mr. Grim get set up. Do I have to wait for them, Mama?"

Her mother brushed a strand of hair out of Anna's face.

"You go on ahead. I know you're keen on getting there early today."

"Thanks, Mama," Anna grabbed her books and her coat, and raced out of the house before Noah and Margaret could protest.

Nellie was waiting for her at the fork. "Hurry up. Mr. Grim left hours ago, and I told him we'd be right along."

As they hurried up the road to the schoolhouse, Anna said, "So? What's he like? Does he seem nice?"

"He's nice enough, I guess, but he's not very sociable. He ate dinner on a tray up in his room, and he stayed up there all evening. Mama says he needs peace and quiet because he's a writer as well as a teacher."

Anna and Nellie got to school about fifteen minutes earlier than usual. They found Mr. Grim standing in the center of the room staring at the wood-burning stove as if he'd never seen one before. The weather had turned cold overnight, and the schoolroom had a chill that would turn their fingers blue.

When he saw them come in the door he gave them a wide smile and cried, "Ah, ladies. I am glad to see you. Would you happen to know where the kindling box is kept?"

"Mrs. Phibbs usually brought the kindling from home. She came early and had the fire roaring by the time we got here," Nellie told him.

"Well, no one told me that starting the fire would be part of my duties, but now I know. Do you suppose we can scrounge up enough to start a blaze?"

"Didn't you have to start the fire at your old school?" Nellie asked.

"Actually, I believe the caretaker did that when he readied the building in the morning. I don't suppose you have a caretaker here, do you?"

Nellie and Anna glanced at each other. Who ever heard of a school having a caretaker?

Anna and Nellie went back outside to look for some kindling and Anna whispered, "He sure is dressed up fine. Do you suppose he'll dress like that every day?"

"That's what city folk do. They always dress that way," she whispered.

They gathered enough kindling to start the fire, and the room was soon warm. Anna and Nellie took their places at the desk they shared and took out their books. Nellie was reading *Elsie Dinsmore* and Anna was reading a book Mr. Jenkins, the lighthouse keeper, had loaned her from his library called *Oliver Twist*, by Charles Dickens. They had been reading only a few minutes when Mr. Grim pulled a stool up to their desk; he had a piece of paper and a pencil with him.

"Excuse me, ladies. I'm afraid I'll need your assistance again."

Anna and Nellie closed their books and gave him their attention. "Yes, Mr. Grim?"

"As you may know, all schools operate differently. Schools in Baltimore, like the one I've come from, may be very different from schools in these parts. I think it best to stick to what you students are used to, so I wonder if you'd mind going over for me what you do each day. That way I'll be able to follow approximately the same schedule as Mrs. . . . ."

"Phibbs," Nellie supplied.

"Yes. Mrs. Phibbs."

"Well, Mrs. Phibbs always began by ringing the bell at 8:30," Anna told him.

"Then the children come to their desks. The girls sit on this side, the boys on that," Nellie explained.

"We say prayers, and she reads from the Bible," Anna went on. "We recite poetry, and then we do arithmetic. Nellie and I work with the young ones on sums, and Mrs. Phibbs worked with the others doing multiplication. Joe Eggle works in the younger group even though he's almost as old as Nellie."

Nellie tapped her forehead. "He's a bit slow."

Mr. Grim kept nodding and wrote down everything they said.

It's almost as though he's the student and we're the teachers, Anna thought. He had a habit of pushing his hair back from his forehead which, strangely enough, reminded her of Toby and made her like him.

Finally he said, "All right. Is there anything else I should know?"

Anna hesitated and, glancing at Nellie, said, "Well, often on cold mornings Mrs. Phibbs would bring in hot cocoa for us."

"Hmmm. Hot cocoa?"

"And sometimes she brought in sweets," Nellie added, even though she had only done that once.

Before they could say any more, Joe Eggle and Clarence Crockett came thumping up the wooden steps of the schoolhouse, and their first day with Mr. Grim began.

Five

All day long the letter burned like a hot coal in Anna's pocket. She could feel it there while she did her reciting and helped Billy Pittman with his sums. She could feel it at recess while she led the younger children in Follow the Leader. Knowing it was there made what was already a strange day even stranger.

The day was strange to begin with because of Mr. Grim. Anna and Nellie agreed that he was the oddest teacher they had ever had.

At lunch Nellie whispered to Anna, "I don't believe he's ever taught before. He doesn't seem to know what to do."

"I know," Anna whispered. "It's a good thing you and I are here to tell him."

"And did you see him when Emmie started to cry? He looked scared."

"And then he gave her his handkerchief!" Nellie exclaimed. "Can you imagine?"

"She's such a crybaby. Mrs. Phibbs would have told her to control herself or she'd be sitting in the dunce seat."

Nellie nodded towards some of the bigger boys who were standing in a knot over by the well. "What do you think they're up to?"

"I don't know," Anna said with a smile, "but I just saw Joe Eggle slip a frog into his pocket."

They laughed. Joe Eggle might have been stupid when it came to lessons, but they had to admit he was good at thinking up pranks. He had livened up lots of boring afternoons, much to Mrs. Phibbs's despair.

After school, as they walked down the schoolhouse lane, Nellie said, "Want to come to my house? I'll show you my new dress designs."

Nellie was forever drawing dresses, copying them from her mother's catalogues. She would add a flounce here or a ruffle there and call them her own designs. To Anna, who didn't care a whit about fashion, it seemed a silly occupation, but Nellie could spend hours doing nothing else.

"I can't," Anna told her. "Mama wants me home to help with the jelly-making."

This wasn't exactly true, but she hadn't told Nellie about what had been going on with the notes and the letter from Toby, and she wasn't sure she was ready to yet. She could have invited her to go along with her down to the old lighthouse, but she wanted to go alone. The time would come to tell Nellie, but not yet.

When they came to the road that led down to her house, Nellie said, "Tonight I'm going to keep my eye on Mr. Grim.

There's something very odd about him, and I intend to find out what's going on."

Anna nodded. "Yes. See what you can find out. But don't let your Mama catch you spying on him."

"Ha, don't worry about that. I wouldn't dare let Mama catch me. She'd have a conniption fit if she thought I was spying on one of our paying guests."

"See you tomorrow," Anna called as Nellie started down the road.

Anna began to run, in a hurry now to get to the old lighthouse that stood at the very end of the point. It had only been five years since the new lighthouse was built, and the old one taken out of service. The building was just now beginning to show signs of disrepair and peeling paint, but still it stood proudly on the point. It reminded Anna of a retired captain, stripped of his duties, but still proud and full of dignity.

The shoals had shifted several years back, and boats had started running aground out in what used to be the middle of the channel. They had built the new lighthouse at the end of the shoals, and Mr. Jenkins had moved out there.

It seemed like a lonely life to Anna, being way out there, alone most of the time, but Mr. Jenkins said it suited him. The new lighthouse was a screw pile type, an octagonal house built on a scaffolding of iron pilings and crossbars. It was a snug little house, and Mr. Jenkins kept it neat and clean as a ship's cat. It seemed to Anna that he was always painting or scrubbing or whitewashing something or other. And the truth was, he really wasn't very far offshore, only a short row in his little punt. Not like some of the stories he told about lighthouse keepers who lived miles offshore, sometimes on tiny islands clear out in the middle of the ocean.

Mr. Jenkins was full of stories, and he loved it when Anna and Nellie visited him. They would sit on the wooden deck that ran around the outside of the lighthouse and Mr. Jenkins would tell them stories while he carved or painted or scrubbed.

Another thing Anna loved about Mr. Jenkins was that he always had books from the Lighthouse Service. The tender boat came around, bringing orders for the keepers, food and necessities, and books if you requested them. Mr. Jenkins said that lots of the keepers didn't hold with reading much of anything besides the Bible, but he had found that a good book helped to pass many a lonely evening. A few years ago, when he noticed that Anna was interested in his books, he began to let her borrow them. She had read all kinds of things thanks to Mr. Jenkins.

Besides his duties as keeper of the new lighthouse, Mr. Jenkins was in charge of keeping an eye on the old one too. He knew that Anna and Toby, and sometimes Nellie, went there and used it as their private place, and he didn't mind, as long as they didn't go upstairs and didn't hurt anything.

"Lord knows, somebody might as well visit her," he said, as if the lighthouse were a lonely old friend.

Today as she set off on the footpath across the marsh that led to the old lighthouse, Anna thought about the last time she and Toby had come here. It had been right before he left. They hadn't been coming much in the last year, and if Anna went there, it was usually with Nellie, rather than Toby. But that morning Toby had said, "Meet me at the old lighthouse after you get out of school. I want to tell you something," and Anna had known right away that he had something important to talk about.

When she went down to the point after school he was there already, waiting for her.

"I'm going oystering," he told her. "On a drudge boat."

Anna stared at him. "A drudge? Whose?"

"Captain Jake Neville. Out of Crisfield. He's coming to the docks tonight to pick me up."

"Does Pa know?"

"Pa?" he said with a laugh. "You think I'd be going if Pa knew?"

"Hmm. I guess not. But why?" she asked him.

He frowned. "Everyone's going to be drudging soon. It's the only way. You can get so many oysters, make so much money. Pa's crazy. He'll never be able to keep up by tonging."

It was a familiar argument. Anna had heard it all at the dinner table time and time again. Her father was a tonger, catching oysters the old way, from a small boat on the shoals, with a long-handled rakelike tool. It was hard work, but her father and his father and his grandfather had all made a good living tonging for oysters. But now the drudge boats were taking over. They were large sailing vessels that pulled a heavy metal scoop across the oyster beds. According to her father, they were depleting the oyster supply, and stealing the oysters that rightfully belonged to the tongers. There were laws that prohibited drudgers from oystering on the shoals and in shallow water, but many of the drudgers paid no attention to those laws. Her father hated the drudgers.

"Pa'll have a fit when he finds out."

"But by then I'll be gone. And when I come back I'll have lots of money. He won't hate that," Toby said.

"But Toby, some of those drudgers are dangerous. You've heard the stories."

The drudgers had a bad reputation. There were stories of drudge captains starving their crew, and even of paying them off with the boom (pushing them overboard into the freezing waters of the Chesapeake miles from shore) when it came time to divide up the profits.

"Those are just stories, rumors. The tongers hate the drudgers because they make more money, so they spread rumors. Most of them are lies. And Captain Jake seems like a good captain."

Anna knew Toby well enough to realize that there was no stopping him. He had made up his mind, and nothing she could say would change it. He was going, and all she could do was pray.

The next morning he was gone, and that was the last she heard of him until she got the three strange messages, and then the letter that she couldn't read.

When she came to the lighthouse, Anna lifted and turned the little brass ring and pushed open the wooden door. Inside, the lighthouse was the same as ever, dark and damp and dusty. There was a pile of old blankets that she and Toby had brought, and some crates that they used for furniture. Everything was the same as they had left it the day Toby told her he was shipping out on the drudge boat.

Anna went to the bottom of the iron staircase and stood facing the window that looked out over the Bay. Then she

paced off eight steps. She stopped and knelt, inspecting the dusty wooden floorboards.

There it was, the loose board. Using her fingernails, she pried the board up and swept the dirt from beneath it to expose the top of a metal tin they had buried years ago when she and Toby had first started coming here.

She pulled the tin out of the ground and opened it. It held treasures of all kinds, secrets that she and Toby had shared, things they wanted to keep hidden from their parents and the younger children. There was Toby's collection of arrowheads, and her collection of beach glass, the letters that Nellie Perry's cousin wrote to her after they met last summer. And there was a little bag of tobacco and rolling papers, and plugs of chewing tobacco that Toby had begun experimenting with.

Anna put the letter in it, replaced the lid, and put the box back in the ground. She covered it up with dirt and then put the floorboard back, fitting it carefully into place so that no one could tell it was loose. It would be safe there until she had figured out what she was going to do.

When Anna got back from the lighthouse her mother was in the kitchen baking an apple pie. She handed Anna a basket and said, "Go on out to the garden and pick us some squash for supper, would you please, Anna?"

"Yes, Mama," Anna said. She took the basket and went out quickly, glad that her mother hadn't noticed she was late coming home from school.

As she walked across the yard to the vegetable garden a flock of Canada geese passed overhead, honking noisily.

Anna smiled. She loved the geese. Maybe they would stop in the marsh beyond the yard, settling down in a big bunch for the night. Their honking always sounded to Anna as if they were arguing, a big noisy family trying to decide what route to take and where to stop for the night.

As she watched the geese, she noticed that the sky was turning pink, the sun nearly set, though it was only a little past five. The days were getting shorter now that it was the end of October. Soon there would be frost every morning, and in a few weeks they might even get their first bit of snow. She thought of Toby out on the Bay and shivered. She had listened to the watermen yarning as they sat around the woodstove at Crick's, telling tales of mornings so cold and damp that their gloves would freeze onto the tong shafts. Or sometimes, on a drudge boat, they would lose their grip on the crank handle and it would spin out of control, knocking the oystermen clear across the deck, and sometimes right off the boat and into the icy Chesapeake.

When she got to the garden Anna saw Noah on the edge of the marsh, fussing with one of the traps that he and Toby had built. She waved and he came over to her, frowning.

"What's wrong with you?" she asked him. "You look as glum as Willy when he's been left behind."

"It's that no-account muskrat trap. You couldn't catch a blind squirrel with that thing," he grumbled. "I wish Toby was here. He'd know how to fix it."

"I don't know why you want to catch the poor little animals anyhow. They're not hurting you any."

Noah scrunched up one side of his face and peered at her the way he always did when he was thinking. Finally he shook his head. "You wouldn't understand. When's Toby coming back, anyhow?" he asked.

"Mama told you last night. No one knows for sure."

Noah picked up a pine cone and flung it hard into the woods. "Well, I don't see why he had to go off with a drudger. Why couldn't he just stay here and work with Pa? I wish Pa would let me go out with him."

"He will when you get a little older. You got to learn to read and write first."

"I know." He was quiet for a minute. "I just wish Toby would come home soon," he said.

"I know," Anna told him. "I miss him too."

Six

"There's something odd about Mr. Grim," Nellie said to Anna as they walked to school the next day. The younger children had run ahead. Anna could see Noah and Thomas swinging their books around. The boys all carried their books in a strap, but the girls used cloth book bags that they sewed themselves. Anna and Nellie were walking slowly, swinging their book bags, in no hurry to get there early this morning.

"What do you mean?" Anna asked.

"Well, for one thing, he hardly ever comes out of his room. He just stays up there. He even takes his meals up there."

"What does he do up there all the time?"

Nellie shrugged. "Mama says writers are like that. Solitary, she says."

Anna nodded. "I believe that's true. Writers need peace and quiet to collect their thoughts," she said.

"But that's not the only thing that's strange," Nellie told her.

"Well? What else?"

"Last night, very late, after Thomas and I were in bed, and even after Mama was in bed, I heard him leave the cottage."

"Perhaps he just felt like taking some fresh air," Anna said.

"Perhaps, but it is rather odd, don't you think? To stay locked away upstairs all evening, and only go out in the middle of the night, long after everyone else is in bed?"

"It is peculiar," Anna agreed. "Did you see where he went? Did he take a walk, or sit on the porch, or what?"

"I don't know. I just heard him leave. I tried to stay awake until he came back, but I must have fallen asleep. Next thing I knew, it was morning."

They had come to the schoolyard where some of the children were already waiting for Mr. Grim to ring the bell. Before they went into the yard Nellie stopped and grabbed Anna's arm. "Let's keep our eye on him today and see if he does anything out of the ordinary. I'm telling you, there's something queer about him."

Anna nodded. "We'll watch him," she whispered.

In a minute Mr. Grim stepped out on the steps of the schoolhouse and began to ring the big brass school bell. The children in the yard stopped their games and raced for the steps, elbowing each other out of the way, and the few who were still straggling up the lane broke into a run so as not to be late.

When they were all settled in their desks, Mr. Grim read a selection from the Bible, and then asked Alma Crick to lead them in prayers. When the opening exercises were finished, he told them to take out some work, and, looking at his watch, announced that he had an errand to run. "Anna, would you watch the class for a few minutes?"

"Yes, Mr. Grim," Anna said.

"I won't be long," he said, and he strode down the aisle and was gone before they knew what had happened. Anna looked at Nellie. Never in all the years she attended the school had their teacher left the classroom. Once or twice Mrs. Phibbs had dismissed class early, but she had never ever just waltzed out in the middle of school leaving the children staring after her.

Anna took *Oliver Twist* and went to sit in Mr. Grim's seat, as he had indicated she should. Most of the other children took out their McGuffey's and began to read to themselves.

For a few minutes, peace and quiet reigned. Then Anna felt rather than saw a wave of commotion in the back of the boys' side of the room. Something was going on back there. Anna stared at them, but they were still, pretending to be engrossed in their books. She went back to reading, but as soon as she looked down, the commotion started up again. She raised her head and it stopped. This continued for a few minutes. What were those boys doing? She couldn't tell.

Finally Anna stood up and walked back to where they were sitting. Elmer quickly shoved something in his pocket and took up his book, but not before Anna had managed to see a tiny bit of fur.

"What is it, Elmer? I know you've got an animal or something in there."

"Huh?" Elmer looked up at her innocently.

"Come on, Elmer. If you show me what you've got, I won't tell Mr. Grim."

He folded his lips together and gave Anna a slant-eyed glance. "Promise?"

"Promise."

"Okay." He reached into his pocket and pulled out a tiny ball of fur no bigger than an orange. "It's a baby kitten," he said, holding the frightened little creature in the palm of his hand and stroking its soft fur with one finger. "He must'a gotten lost from his mother because he was just sittin' outside on the grass, too skeered even to run away."

"Poor baby," Anna put both hands out and Elmer gently transferred the kitten to her hands. "You kin hold him for a minute, but no one else. He's already skeered enough."

"It's okay little one," Anna crooned. "We'll take care of you." His little kitten ears lay flat against his head, and his round green eyes were wide with fear.

"Now it's turning cold outside," Elmer went on, "and this little kitty's like to freeze to death."

Anna looked out at the cold gray day. The weather had changed in the last few days. Indian summer was gone, and the days had turned cold and gray, with a bone-chilling wind. "Poor little kitty," she murmured, stroking its soft fur.

The other children gathered around trying to get a look at him. Anna handed him back to Elmer. "Let everyone take turns getting a look at him, Elmer," Anna said. "Everyone line up and you can all get a chance to pet him."

The children lined up behind Elmer's desk, and one by one they put out a finger and stroked the little kitten. When

Mr. Grim came back a few minutes later, not one person except Elmer was in his seat.

Anna was afraid he'd be furious. "Umm, we, umm," she began stammering out an explanation, "Elmer found a baby kitten, and—"

"A kitten?" he asked. "Let's see."

The children moved aside and Elmer held out the kitten.

"I see. Tiny little thing, isn't he?"

"I was just letting all the children have a look," Anna explained. "That's why they're all out of their seats."

"Yes. Well, that seems fair. I'm sure they all wanted to see it," Mr. Grim said. "Now I suppose we'll have to find out what to do with him. Does anyone know anything about the care of kittens?"

The rest of the morning was spent making a home for the kitten out of a box and learning about the care and feeding of baby kittens.

At lunchtime in the schoolyard, all the children were whispering about how different school was and how much fun, now that Mr. Grim was here.

"We've never had a teacher like him before," Alma said happily, "have we?"

"He's different, all right," Nellie said, giving Anna a knowing look. "He sure is different."

As soon as school was out, Anna caught up to Nellie and said, "Come with me to Crick's. I told Mama I'd get the mail."

Mr. Crick's store was warm and thick with the smell of smoke from the woodstove. A few of the watermen sat in the back of the store playing checkers near the stove. Her pa would not be there yet, Anna knew. Even in the worst weather he would stay out as long as the light held, filling his boat as full as could be with oysters. Everyone knew her pa was the most determined waterman on the Eastern Shore. He went out in all kinds of weather, oystering on the coldest of days and crabbing on the hottest. "If your pa ain't catchin' 'em, ain't no one catchin' 'em," old Captain Shanahan always told her.

Crick's was busy today, and Anna and Nellie had to wait in line for the mail. They waited while Mrs. Riggens debated about the merits of Dr. Barkham's Curative or Pinkham's Elixir as a remedy for her cold. They waited while Mr. Crick cut a plug of tobacco for Mr. Crockett, and they waited while Mrs. Constable found a button to match the ones on Mr. Constable's good coat.

Finally it was their turn. "I'm sure I know what you ladies are waiting for," Mr. Crick told them. "Nellie, your Mama picked up your mail already, but there's something here for you, Anna," he said, and he handed her a familiar-looking envelope addressed to Miss Anna Shipherd.

Anna took the envelope and said, "Thanks, Mr. Crick." She knew when she saw it that it was from Aunt Phoebe.

"What is it, Anna?" Nellie asked.

"It's from Aunt Phoebe. She wants me to come to school up in Baltimore. She said she'd write and tell me all about it."

"Aren't you going to open it?" Nellie asked.

"Not yet. I'll wait till tonight. If I can find some privacy," she said.

"Are you going to go?" Nellie asked.

"I don't know yet. I want to, but . . ."

"You're scared?"

Scared? Was that it? Anna hated to think that she was scared, but when she really thought about it, that's what it was. "Pa doesn't like the idea. He doesn't believe in education, so . . . I don't know. I have to think about it."

"Well, I think you should go. Baltimore! A fancy school. You have to go."

"We'll see."

Anna tucked the envelope into her book bag. She and Nellie had started down the steps of the store when Anna's eye was caught by a movement down near the marsh. Two figures stood there, two dark silhouettes, black against the misty gray marsh. One was dressed in oilskins and a black cap. "It's him!" Anna cried, grabbing Nellie's arm and pulling her down the road, out of sight of the men.

"Who?" Nellie asked. "What are you talking about?"

But Anna just stared. She was too shocked to speak. The other figure was wearing a dress coat and boots and carried an umbrella. It was Mr. Grim.

"Anna? What is it? What's wrong?"

"Ssshh. Quickly, come with me. We can't talk now. Let's go to the lighthouse and I'll tell you everything."

"That's Mr. Grim, isn't it? Do you know something about him? Who's that man he's talking to?"

"Not now. We'll talk when we get to the lighthouse," Anna said and she started running.

Why was Mr. Grim talking to the man with oyster hand? Was he in league with him somehow? Was that why he'd been sneaking out of Nellie's house late at night? And what did it all have to do with her?

"Aaannnna," Nellie cried, "wait for me."

But Anna didn't slow down. She ran as fast as she could. Anna had always been a strong, fast runner, faster than all the girls and most of the boys she knew. Today she ran her fastest, as if she could outrun the jumble of confused thoughts that were swirling through her brain.

 *Seven*

Anna kept on running, past the fork that led to the Perrys', past her own road, and right on to the end of the point and down the path that led to the old lighthouse. She ran past the line of cedar trees on the shore; but when she was just about ten feet from the lighthouse, she stopped. She stopped so suddenly that Nellie ran right into her and almost bowled her over.

"What? What's wrong?" Nellie demanded.

Anna stood perfectly still, staring at the lighthouse.

"Someone's been here, I think."

"How do you know? I don't see anyone."

Something looked different. What was it? Anna asked herself. Then she saw the thin black slit between the white door and the white wall of the lighthouse. Someone had left the door just the tiniest bit ajar. Anna was always careful to shut it up tight to keep out rain and small animals.

"Maybe Mr. Jenkins came by," Nellie said.

"Maybe," Anna said. She moved cautiously to the door.

She stopped and listened, but heard nothing except the lapping of waves and the cry of an osprey from across the water.

Tentatively, Anna lifted the round brass ring and pushed. The heavy wooden door swung open and Anna and Nellie stepped into the cold and dank interior of the lighthouse.

Anna crossed quickly to her hiding place beneath the floorboards. She pried the loose board up, scraped away the dirt, and pulled out the tin box.

"Lordy, Anna. I never knew that was under there."

"No, and you wouldn't be knowing it now except that I've got to tell someone."

"Tell someone what?"

Anna opened the box and lifted the envelope out. She took the letter out of the envelope and showed it to Nellie.

"Yesterday this came in the mail for me."

Nellie took the letter from Anna and unfolded it. She studied it for a minute. "What language is it?" she asked. Anna shrugged. "I think maybe Mr. Jenkins will know. I'm going to show it to him."

"Who sent it? And who was the man with Mr. Grim? What's going on, Anna?" Nellie asked.

"I don't really know," Anna began. "But it's got something to do with Toby."

Anna told Nellie all about the messages and the man who had stared at her in Crick's and was lurking outside her house that night. "It was the same man I just saw talking to Mr. Grim," she said.

"Really?" Nellie's eyes widened. "Are you sure?"

Anna nodded. "It was him all right," she said with a shiver. "He gives me the willies."

"But what was Mr. Grim doing with him?"

Anna shrugged. "Like you said, there's something odd about Mr. Grim."

"He sure does have a strange way of teaching," Nellie agreed. Nellie wrapped her arms tightly around her chest and gave a little shake. "Ooh, it's creepy! Poor Toby! What are you going to do?"

"I don't know," Anna said. "All I know is I've got to do something before I go crazy."

"If we hurry we can still get to Mr. Jenkins' before we have to be home," Nellie told her. "Is the dory on your beach?"

"I think so," Anna said, folding the letter and putting it back in the envelope and tucking the envelope into her book bag.

"Then let's go," Nellie said.

Nellie helped Anna put the tin box back in its hiding spot and cover it up. As they left the lighthouse Anna made sure to close the door tight behind them.

A few minutes later they were rowing towards Heron Light in the little dory that the Shipherds kept on the beach. Most of the watermen had finished for the day, but a few boats still bobbed on the water, white sails full in the brisk, late afternoon breeze.

The wind was cold and blew right through Anna. She was glad when they reached the rock pile that surrounded the lighthouse.

Mr. Jenkins was out on the deck of the lighthouse painting. When he saw them coming across the water, he raised his paintbrush and then stood with a smile, watching them as they drew closer.

When they were close enough to hear him he said, "Looka there, someone's coming to see me. Look kinda familiar, but I don't recollect who they may be . . ." He scratched his head in a puzzled way. It was a game they had played since Anna was not much older than Margaret, Mr. Jenkins always make-believing he didn't recognize her because it had been so long between visits.

"Oh, Mr. Jenkins, it hasn't been that long," Anna said. "Why, Toby and I came just a few weeks ago."

"A few weeks. That's a long time. A man gets lonely way out here on the water."

"Oh, pshaw, Mr. Jenkins. You get more visitors out here than the mayor does, and you know it."

"Huh. I see I get more sympathy out of that rock there than I do out of you gals," he said, as he caught the line Anna threw him and tied it to the metal ring set into the rocks.

Anna stowed the oars and she and Nellie stepped carefully out of the little boat and up onto the rocks. They followed Mr. Jenkins through the gate in the railing and onto the deck of the lighthouse.

"Looks like you've been doing some painting," Anna said.

"That I have, that I have. Finishing up this trim work. You don't mind if I keep at it while we talk, do you?" he asked, dipping his brush into the bucket of paint.

"It sure looks nice," Anna said, looking at the newly bright white trim around the windows and door.

She leaned against the railing and took a deep breath, smelling the familiar smells of the lighthouse: fresh paint, lamp oil, and brass polish mingling with the salty air.

"Weather's mighty hard on a paint job out here. Seems as soon as I finish it's time to start all over."

"Where are Sam and Penelope?" Anna asked, looking around for Mr. Jenkins's two tame sea gulls that were almost always somewhere nearby.

"They took off in a huff. Sam was messing with my paint. Stuck his foot in it and left tracks on the deck. Looka here," and he pointed to sea gull footprints on the gray deck, and Anna and Nellie laughed.

"I yelled at him, and he and Penelope went off somewhere to sulk. But they'll be back when they get hungry, sure as you're alive."

Mr. Jenkins began painting the rim of a window in neat even strokes. "So, tell me what's going on on the mainland. Am I missing anything?"

Anna wondered where to start. She wanted to tell him everything, but could she? Should she? "You heard about Toby, I guess," she began.

"Oh, yes. That's old news. And it don't surprise me much. That rascal was spoiling for some adventure. I guess your daddy's not too happy about it, though."

"He sure isn't."

"How's it going for Toby? You heard anything from him?"

"Well, sort of," she said.

Mr. Jenkins turned to look at her. He adjusted the brim of his hat and studied Anna's face. "You worried?"

Anna nodded. She told him about the notes and pulled out the letter. "And then this came."

Mr. Jenkins took it from her and studied it. "Hmm," he

said finally. "Came in the mail, did it?"

Anna nodded. "Yesterday," she told him. "And it looks like Toby's handwriting on the envelope."

"German," he said. "This is German. Where would Toby get a letter written in German? And why would he send it to you?"

"That's what I want to know," Anna said. "Can you read German, Mr. Jenkins?"

"I'm afraid I can't, but . . ." he paused, gazing out to sea with an absent expression.

"But what?" Anna prompted.

"Well, Dora used to correspond with a German woman, and she had a German dictionary. Maybe I can puzzle out some of the meaning."

"Could you? I'd be so grateful. I don't know what to think about it all," Anna cried.

Mr. Jenkins folded the letter. "Well, I'll give it a try. I can't make any promises, but I'll do my best."

"You keep it, then. I . . . I think it might be safer out here with you," Anna said.

Mr. Jenkins took the letter and tucked it into the pocket of his overalls. "I'll see what I can do. Come back tomorrow and maybe I'll have some idea what this letter is all about."

A sea gull squawked and Mr. Jenkins smiled. "Look there," he said.

Anna and Nellie looked where he was pointing and saw Sam and Penelope flying towards the lighthouse. "I told you those rascals would be back when they got hungry."

Eight

Everything was cold, damp, and hard. Movement was impossible. Darkness was everywhere. The smell of rot, excrement, death. The sound of scrabbling, rodents drawing closer, moving in, biding their time—

Anna woke, her heart pounding and her skin damp with sweat. She lay frozen with terror, the nightmare wrapping cold fingers of fear around her. She was too scared to move at first, until gradually the sounds of Margaret's soft even breathing and Noah's light snores comforted her and the warmth and safety of the loft enveloped her. Her heart slowed, and the nightmare began to recede into the netherlands of her mind. But she was wide awake. She couldn't face going back to sleep, back to that horrible dream.

The loft was bright with the silvery light of the moon. Anna slid out from under the quilt carefully, so that she wouldn't wake Margaret, and tiptoed across the floor to the window. All the leaves were gone from the trees now, and the bare black branches of the locusts on the shoreline bent against the stiff wind. Anna looked past the trees, out onto the shoals, and saw the boat. Somehow she had known it would be there—a drudger, drudging for oysters on her father's shoals. They were stealing her father's oysters under the cover of night, because they knew it was illegal for drudgers to work the shoals.

Toby was on that boat. Anna knew it surer than she knew her father would shoot them all if he caught them out there. Toby was on that boat, but he was a prisoner. He was in the nightmare; only for him it wasn't just a dream, it was real. Anna began to tremble. He was out there, so close, yet unreachable. And she had to help him.

Her trembling grew stronger and she sank to her knees. Her cheeks were wet with tears as she lay her head on her arms and wept, the terror she had felt in the nightmare threatening to overwhelm her. And then she began to pray.

Please God, she prayed, tell me what to do. The fear receded, and in its place came a firm resolve. She would rescue Toby. She could. She had to.

Finally she was able to return to her bed and fall back to sleep, but it was a fitful, uneasy sleep, and she woke next morning feeling achy and worried. Noah and Margaret had left for school while Anna was still dressing, but somehow she was unable to make herself hurry.

She got to school just as Mr. Grim finished ringing the bell and she had no chance to talk to Nellie before class. Nellie was sitting in the back of the room, working with some of the younger children on their sums, while Anna read to another group. But halfway through the morning, Emma

Lou Baines dropped an acorn cap into Anna's lap and whispered, "From Nellie," as she passed her desk. Anna's fingers
closed over the acorn and she looked back at Nellie and
nodded. It was their signal to meet at the oak tree on the
edge of the schoolyard at lunchtime.

Anna thought that lunchtime would never arrive, but
finally the morning passed and Mr. Grim dismissed them for
lunch.

Nellie was one of the first out the door. Anna took her
lunch pail, but she didn't want to follow too closely behind
Nellie for fear someone would see them trying to have a
private meeting and decide to spy on them. It would be just
like Elmer Crockett and the rest of the boys to try to listen
in when she and Nellie wanted to have a private conversation. Sometimes it didn't really matter, but today they
weren't just discussing who had a crush on who, or how Nellie
was going to get Billy Macalroy, the blacksmith's son, to
notice her. Today was serious, and the last thing they needed
was anyone overhearing them.

She waited until the boys were involved in a game of
Crack the Whip, and then, when she thought no one was
watching, she snuck off to join Nellie behind the big oak.

Nellie looked around to make sure no one could hear her,
and then she whispered, "Anna, I think Mr. Grim is involved
with the oyster drudgers somehow."

"What do you mean?" Anna asked her.

"Well, last night, when I carried his dinner tray up to his
room, I managed to get a look at a letter he was writing,"
Nellie paused to measure the effect of her words on Anna.

"And?" Anna prompted.

"Well, I couldn't see much, but I could see the words 'oyster' and 'drudger.' Whatever it was that he was writing had something to do with oystering. And we saw him talking to that creepy man. We saw him with our own eyes. Do you think he's involved in all this somehow?"

"All what?" Anna asked. "We don't even know what's going on. All we know is that Toby's in trouble." Anna shivered, remembering her dream from the night before.

"What?" Nellie said when she saw Anna shivering. "What about Toby?"

"Nothing, just . . . just I've got to think of a way to help him. He's in trouble; I know it."

"Mr. Jenkins might be able to help us. Let's go back out to the lighthouse this afternoon and see if he's found out anything from the letter."

"Yes. Let's go the minute school is out."

"Okay, but I promised Mama I'd stop in town and pick up some things at Crick's. I'll come right after that."

"I'll wait for you at the old lighthouse. Come as soon as you can," Anna said, as Mr. Grim stepped out on the front steps of the school and rang the bell to signal the end of lunch.

All afternoon as she sat at her desk, helping some of the younger children with their letters, Anna thought about what Nellie had told her. Was Mr. Grim connected somehow to the oysterman she had seen near her house? Why had he been talking to him? And why had he been writing about drudgers? What was the connection? And was it related to Toby somehow? None of it made sense. Maybe Mr. Jenkins could help her figure it all out.

The minute school was out, Anna headed for the old lighthouse. She was kind of glad that Nellie couldn't come right away. She wanted a few minutes to herself to think.

But as soon as she got to the lighthouse she knew that someone had been there again. This time they hadn't tried to hide it. The door stood wide open, and there were footprints in the mud all along the path. Mr. Jenkins? she thought. But he would never leave the door open like that.

She slowed down as she approached the lighthouse, stopping a few feet from the open doorway. She listened. Maybe whoever it was was still in there. Fear swept over her. The face of the man with oyster hand floated before her, cruel and menacing. Was he in there waiting for her?

Slowly she crept towards the doorway, listening for sounds of anyone inside. She heard nothing, and when she came close enough she peered in and saw that the room was empty.

But someone had been there. That much was obvious. Someone had been looking for something. The blankets that Anna and Toby had left there were thrown on the floor, and the crates that they used for tables and benches were turned over. Anna crossed quickly to her hiding place beneath the floorboards and saw that someone had found it. The boards had been pulled aside and the tin taken out and left lying open on the ground, as if someone had flung it there in a fury when they found it empty.

What were they looking for? Did someone know about the letter? How had they found her hiding place?

Nine

Her heart pounded with terror as she stood staring at the empty tin box. She had left it covered up in the hole, but someone had discovered it. Were they watching her? What did they want?

Thank God she had given the letter to Mr. Jenkins. Would they try to get it from him? Would they ransack his lighthouse?

Dream images from the night before kept surfacing in her mind and it was hard to hold her fear at bay. She felt like running, tearing away from the lighthouse, back up the path to the safety of her house. But she couldn't do that. She had to wait for Nellie and then they would go see Mr. Jenkins. Time was growing short. She had to rescue Toby soon.

Anna sat just outside the lighthouse, waiting for Nellie. Her heart was still pounding. She tried to keep calm but it was impossible. What if they were right there in the woods, watching her? Where was Nellie? Why didn't she hurry up?

Finally Anna saw her coming down the path. She stood up and ran to her.

"They've been here," Anna told her in a shaky voice. "They ransacked the place and found our hiding spot."

"They found the tin box under the boards?" Nellie asked.

Anna nodded. "They found it. Thank God we gave the letter to Mr. Jenkins. We've got to go out there right now. I'm so worried about Toby. . ."

"Come on; let's go."

In minutes they were in the Shipherds' dory, rowing towards Mr. Jenkins's lighthouse. A gull swooped towards them and cried a greeting as they came close. "It's Sam," Anna cried. "Hi, Sam. Where's Penelope?"

Sam circled and flew towards the lighthouse as if leading them there.

They tied the boat up, and clambered over the rocks to the walkway that led to the deck. "Mr. Jenkins?" they called.

From the tower came a strange voice. "Ahoy! Who's there?"

"It's us. Anna Shipherd and Nellie Perry. We're friends of Mr. Jenkins."

"Hold on a minute." They heard someone coming down the ladder and a young man appeared on the deck. He was tall and skinny with a thin, bony face and short blond hair. "I'm Ben. I'm Mr. Jenkins's new assistant. He had to go up to Baltimore for a few days, so I'm here to look after things."

Anna's heart sank. Mr. Jenkins was gone? Why had he gone to Baltimore? He hadn't said anything about taking a trip. Now what? Who else could help them?

Nellie looked at her. "Do you think it had something to do with the letter?" she whispered.

"Did he say why he had to go?" Anna asked.

The young man shrugged his shoulders. "He didn't say and I didn't ask. He's the captain. T'aint my place to question the captain."

"Okay. Well, do you know when he's coming back?"

Again the man shrugged. "Shouldn't think he'll be away more than a day or two, but I cain't say for certain."

Anna felt a crazy urge to shake the young man and try to get him to tell them something. But it's not his fault, she thought. He doesn't know anything about it.

"We might as well head back," Anna said to Nellie.

Nellie nodded, but she looked as disappointed as Anna felt. "Just tell him we stopped by to see him," Anna told Ben as they headed down the walkway to the rocks.

"I'll sure do that," Ben called after them.

They untied the boat and shoved it away from the rocks.

"Well, he was about as helpful as a clam stuck in the mud," Anna said.

Nellie nodded, staring at Ben as he stood on the deck watching them row off. "He is kind of cute, though. How old do you think he is?"

"For heaven's sake, Nellie. Is that all you can think about?"

"Sorry. I'm just curious, is all."

Anna fought down her anger and fear. She couldn't blame Nellie. She hadn't had the dream that Anna had last night. She didn't understand, couldn't understand. "I know. It's just . . . I'm really scared. I had this dream last night . . ."

"About Toby?" Nellie asked.

Anna nodded. "It . . . He's really in trouble. I . . ." she shivered. She couldn't explain the dream, couldn't articulate the horror it made her feel. Couldn't explain how she knew

Toby was in bad trouble. But she did her best to explain it to Nellie. And she told her about seeing the oyster boat on the shoals last night. Nellie had grown up with the two of them. She understood as well as anyone could.

"It's almost like it's happening to you, isn't it?" Nellie said quietly, her voice full of sympathy.

"Yes. Yes, that's it." She was so grateful to Nellie for understanding.

"Do you think you should tell your parents?" Nellie asked.

"I can't. You know my father. He's so mad at Toby we can't even mention his name. And if he finds out that oyster boat is out there stealing oysters, he might just take a shotgun and start blasting." Anna shook her head. "No, I can't tell them."

"So I guess we just wait for Mr. Jenkins," Nellie said.

At home things were the same as always. Ma was in the kitchen making applesauce with the last of the apples, and Noah and Margaret were playing with cornhusks. They were supposed to be making dolls but Noah kept turning his into monsters and making Margaret cry. Anna threw her book bag on the rocking chair and sat down on the floor to comfort Margaret.

When Pa came in a few minutes later he headed for the rocking chair to take off his workboots. He shoved Anna's book bag out of the chair onto the floor and sat down. The letter from Aunt Phoebe fell out, right beside Noah. He grabbed it and yelled, "A letter! Who's it from, Anna?"

Pa looked up before Anna could grab the letter and tell Noah to shut up.

"Let me see that, son," he said.

Noah took the letter to Pa with a glance at Anna to see how she was reacting. She gave him a look that said, "I'll get you for this."

Her father studied the letter, his brow wrinkled and his lips pursed. "From Phoebe. You seen this, Ma?" he asked.

Anna's mother pretended nonchalance. "Well, Anna mentioned it to me."

"So you knew about this?"

"Yes. I don't see any harm thinking about further schooling for Anna. And this school Phoebe mentions is supposed to be excellent."

"Well, I see plenty of harm. You know as well as I do that Baltimore's a center of sin. And all this book learning for a girl makes no sense. It's the devil's work." He opened the woodstove and dropped the letter inside.

Anna stood up and ran up to the loft. She lay on her back on her pallet, staring at the ceiling. She thought of the game she and Toby used to play, when they would throw dried beans at the knots in the wood and see who could make a bull's eye.

Finally she understood why Toby had done what he had done. There was no other way. She loved her father, but she had to get away from him, and she saw that Toby had had no choice either. If they wanted to have their own life, they had to leave.

It was only the letter he had burned. She could still write to Aunt Phoebe. Somehow, instead of causing her to give up thinking about school in Baltimore, her father's actions had made her see what she should do. Now she knew she had to go, and she would find a way.

Ten

Anna tossed and turned in her bed for what seemed like hours, until finally, afraid that she would wake Margaret if she kept on, she got up and tiptoed to the window.

The wind had died, and outside everything was still and silent, lit by the ghostly light of the moon. The Bay was black and smooth, the moon reflected in a single streak of silver. An oyster moon, her Pa called it. "Farmers call it a harvest moon, but to me it's an oyster moon," he used to say, back when she and Toby were little. He would sometimes take them out with him on a still night like this, and they would catch a few oysters with the nippers and take them home to Ma. The nippers were short-handled tongs used for shallow water. Toby and Anna would take turns with them, seeing who could catch the most. But that was before oysters got so popular, and all the oystermen were fighting all the time.

Anna saw the boat, a ways out on the Bay, and all of a sudden a feeling swept over her, a feeling so strong it almost brought her to her knees. That was Toby's boat. He was out there, right out there, and he was in trouble.

Suddenly, before she had a chance to think about it, Anna knew what she had to do. It was time. She couldn't wait any longer. She couldn't wait for Mr. Jenkins to come back, or for her pa to be in a good mood. She had to do this now, and she had to do it herself. There was no one else.

Anna dressed quietly and hurried down from the loft. Downstairs, Willy was sleeping in his usual spot by the fire. When he heard Anna, he raised his head, gave her a puzzled look, and thumped his tail sleepily.

Anna tiptoed over and knelt down beside him. He put his head in her lap with a contented sigh, and Anna stroked his soft, smooth fur. "It's okay, boy," she whispered. "Everything's okay. I have to go out for a little while, but you have to stay." She kissed the top of his head and gently pushed it off her lap. "Stay, boy. You stay," she whispered firmly.

Anna pulled on a pair of boots and an oilskin coat, and then she tiptoed into the kitchen and took the largest carving knife they owned. As she tucked it into the pocket of the oilskin she prayed she wouldn't have to use it, but she knew she would if she had to.

Willy sat up and gave a soft whine as he watched her move toward the door. Anna knew he wanted to come, but she couldn't let him. "Stay, boy. You stay," she commanded again, and he lay down looking unhappy but resigned.

Silently, Anna left the house. She tiptoed across the porch and down the steps. Once outside, she began to run. She didn't want to stop to think too much about where she was going or what she might find when she got there. If she thought too much about it, she might lose her nerve, and she knew she couldn't let that happen. Toby was in trouble. That was all she knew, except that it was desperate, and there was no one else to help him but her.

Down on the beach she untied the dory, gave it a shove into the water, and stepped in. She sat down and took up the oars, swinging the bow around and pulling hard. There was no wind at all now, which was probably the reason the oyster boat was still out there on the shoals. They had probably come in to steal the oysters and then when the wind died, they were becalmed before they could get back out to the open waters.

It was so still and quiet that Anna felt as if her little boat was gliding along all by itself. The only sounds were the squeak of the oars in the oarlocks and the gentle lapping as she pulled them through the black water.

As she rowed, Anna thought about what she would do when she reached the boat. She prayed that they would be asleep, but she was sure they would have a watch. Someone would be awake or, at least, be supposed to be awake.

As she rowed she concentrated on Toby, trying to send him a mental message that she was on her way. If he knew she was coming, maybe he could be prepared. She wanted to spend as little time as possible on the boat because . . . well, she didn't want to think about what might happen if they caught her.

What would her parents think had happened to her if she wasn't back in the morning? What would they do, how would they find her? If she was still alive, that is.

As she rowed out to the shoals, Anna decided that it was too dangerous to take the dory up to the oyster boat. There was no way she could hide it, and they would be much more likely to hear her. She would have to swim to the boat and that way she could climb aboard silently. Even if there was a watchman awake, she could sneak past him if he weren't alert.

The oyster boat was out on the shoals not too far from the lighthouse. She decided she would leave the dory tied up at the lighthouse and swim to the boat from there. The water was still pretty warm. She knew she could make it. After all, she was the best swimmer in Heron's Harbor.

She tied the dory up at the lighthouse, and took off her boots and her oilskins and her overalls. She would make the swim in her bloomers and her blouse. She took the knife and, using a piece of rope that was lying in the bottom of the dory, fastened it around her waist.

She looked down at the black water. It looked forbidding. Was she crazy? Could she do this? What was down there below the surface, waiting to harm her?

Calm down, she told herself. She had swum in these waters since she was two years old. They were safe. Besides, what choice did she have? She couldn't let Toby die when it was in her power to save him. It would be like a part of herself dying.

She took a deep breath and slipped silently off the rocks, gasping as the cold water surrounded her. She started swimming slowly towards the boat. She didn't want to rush and exhaust herself; she had to conserve her energy. As her body

adjusted to the cold, she began to feel better. She could make it to the boat, and to Toby.

If anyone could see her now they wouldn't believe it, she thought, smiling to herself. Here she was in the middle of the night, in her bloomers, swimming across the shoals. Why hadn't she gotten help, they would ask. Why hadn't she waited? How could she explain it, the force that drove her, the feeling that Toby needed her and needed her now? There was no point in trying to explain it. She just had to do it.

As she slipped smoothly, silently through the water she felt that she was meant to do this. She might have been a seal or a dolphin. She felt in her element. The water had never held fear for her. She had always loved it and felt comfortable in it.

She could feel her arms and legs beginning to tire though, and she still had half the distance to go. She turned on her back and floated for several minutes. The moon was so bright that there weren't many stars, but she saw a few winking in the broad, dark arch of the sky.

She flipped over again and went back to swimming a slow, steady stroke, bringing her closer and closer to the boat and to Toby.

As she came closer she tried to be as silent as possible, slipping through the water without making a sound. The boat loomed before her, huge and forbidding, and she was almost reluctant to reach it, though her limbs were exhausted and the cold was beginning to seep into her bones.

She stopped about ten yards from the boat, treading water and trying to decide the best way to make her approach. No sound came from the boat except the rhythmic clinking of the halyards as the boat rocked gently on the calm water.

The ship's own dory was tied to the stern and Anna realized that she could easily climb into it, and from there get a better view of the decks. She swam to the side of the dory and hauled herself as quietly as she could up over the side of the little boat.

Once in the dory she lay on her back, catching her breath and praying that no one was awake on board the oyster boat. So far she hadn't seen or heard any signs that anyone was awake, but she was sure someone would be on deck on watch. There was always a watch on board a ship at night, but on a calm night like this it was likely that they were asleep too.

When she had caught her breath, Anna sat up and looked at the big ship looming before her. Somewhere inside, Toby waited for her. Did he know she was here, right outside the ship? She felt that he must know, he must sense her presence the way he always had been able to. And now she would have to use that sense of his to find him. He would lead her to him, she felt sure.

Slowly she moved to the bow of the dory and reached for the bow line. Quietly she pulled the dory up to the oyster boat and pulled herself up onto the stern deck of the boat. She crouched in the shadows, her heart pounding in her chest, waiting to see if anyone had heard or seen her. After a few minutes when nothing happened, she stood up and looked around.

Up on the foredeck she saw three men. Two of them were lying down, and one was sitting up as if he was supposed to be on watch, but all of them seemed to be asleep.

There would be more men in the cabin below. Did she dare move across the deck to the cabin? A wave of panic swept over her, and the feeling that she had had after the dream about the dark hole came back stronger than ever. Toby, she thought. He's still in the hole. She had to find him and free him. Slowly, so that she wouldn't make a sound, she crept forward out of the shadows. She stayed close to the side of the boat so that she could crouch and hide if she heard someone coming.

The deck was gritty with sand and mud and oyster shells. As she came amidships she could see the iron handles of the windlass, and the nets and big iron teeth of the dredge itself. A pile of freshly caught oysters was mounded up in the middle of the ship, waiting to be sold to the buy boat the next day.

Just beyond the pile of oysters was the entrance to the cabins below deck. Anna crept forward, stepping carefully so as not to cut her bare feet on an oyster shell. Silently she stole past the windlass and ducked down the steps.

It was very dark in the cabin, and Anna had to wait until her eyes adjusted. In the moonlight that shone through the two portholes she could make out three sleeping bodies in hammocks strung across the width of the cabin. Even in the darkness she could tell that none of them was Toby.

Now what? How was she to find him?

The sleeping hulk closest to Anna twitched, and then an arm was flung out and a noise like thunder erupted from the hulk. Anna grasped the rope handrail, poised for flight, but stood stock still, too scared to breathe. It was merely a snore and the hulk went on sleeping. Anna breathed a sigh of relief, but she knew she had to hurry. At any moment, one of them could wake up.

She closed her eyes and concentrated. Toby, she thought, Toby, where are you? Tell me. Her dream came back to her once again: darkness, pain, and fear. She felt him in her mind, and suddenly she knew where he was.

She went back up the stairs and crept across the deck to the stern. She had probably stepped right over top of him. There was a storage box built into the aft deck, and there, inside, she knew she would find Toby.

With shaking fingers she slid the bolt that locked the box and lifted the lid.

When she saw him, Anna gasped sharply, and covered her mouth quickly to keep herself from crying out. It was him, her beloved Toby, but how different he looked! His face, usually so ruddy and healthy-looking, was pale and sunken, almost skeletal. His hands were bound together with a length of rope, and one hand was swollen and purple with oyster hand. The rest of his body seemed to have shrunk. But it was him.

He was here, and she had found him, and now she was going to get him home.

"Toby! Toby!" she whispered, shaking his shoulder gently.

A desperate wish to be off the boat seized her. She took the knife from where she had tied it around her waist and began to cut the cord which bound his hands. They had to go quickly. Someone would wake up any minute, she was sure of it.

He moaned, opened his eyes briefly, looked at her, but didn't seem to see her, and closed his eyes again. He moved slightly, trying to reposition himself in the tiny space into which he'd been shoved.

"Toby! It's me—Anna. Wake up!" she whispered desperately.

"Anna? Anna," he mumbled, and sank down again into sleep.

He thinks it's a dream, Anna realized.

"Toby." She shook his shoulder. "It's me. I'm really here. Now get up, quickly. We've got to get out of here before they wake up."

His eyes flicked open again, and this time Anna was sure he heard her.

"Toby," she was pulling on his arm, trying to help him get up, when something made her freeze.

Before she could think, a hand grabbed her from behind, and fingers were squeezing her arm so hard she cried out.

She whirled, trying to twist away, but she was caught in a viselike grip. She was looking into the bloodshot eyes of the man who had been spying on her.

Eleven

Panic shot through her as she stared at him. She was too terrified to move.

His lips curled back in a leer and he chuckled softly.

"Well, well, well! Lookahere what I done caught me."

A mangled cry escaped her but he covered her mouth with his hand. "Shhhh. We don't want to wake the others yet, now do we? The captain don't like visitors on his boat."

Waves of fear and revulsion flooded her as she realized she was at the mercy of this horrid man. She could smell his breath, rank and putrid, as he leaned close to her. His greasy hair hung in matted strands around his pock-marked face.

He's drunk, she realized as she watched him swaying and smiling stupidly at her. And in that moment she knew that she could get away from him. She was smaller than he was, but she was also a lot smarter. In a desperate move she kicked him in the groin as hard as she could. He doubled over in pain, and she grabbed the heavy iron bolt that had locked

Toby's box and brought it down on his head as hard as she could.

He fell to the deck in a heap. Anna didn't stop to look at him. She grabbed Toby and yanked him upright. "Wake up!" she commanded.

He sat up and looked at her dazedly. "Anna?"

"Shh. Come on. We have to hurry. Get up," she said, yanking him again. She pulled Toby up, helping him out of the box, and, half supporting him, guided him to the stern of the boat.

"Anna, what . . . "

"Shhh. Don't say anything. Just try to stand here a minute."

As Toby leaned against her, she pulled in the dory and, half guiding, half pushing him, she managed to get him into it.

Then she jumped down into the dory herself, cut the bow line with one swift slicing motion, and cast off. She grabbed the oars and rowed as hard and fast as she could away from the oyster boat.

Toby lay across the stern seat of the little boat. "Anna?" he whispered, peering at her as if he wasn't sure she was real. He sat up and stretched out a hand to touch her. "Anna?"

"Shhh. Not now," Anna told him. She was rowing furiously, desperate to get away from the oyster boat. She didn't want to think about anything but rowing right now. If she let herself think about how terrible Toby looked, or how scared she had been when the man grabbed her, or how she

had actually hit him over the head, she would fall apart. She couldn't let herself think. She just kept rowing, watching the oyster boat grow smaller and smaller the farther away they got.

Finally the lighthouse was in front of them, and in minutes she was pulling the dory up next to the rocks and tying the bow line.

"Wait here," she said to Toby. "I'm going to get help."

She raced up the walkway to the lighthouse and banged on the door. Mr. Jenkins was probably still in Baltimore, she thought. His assistant Ben would help, but she wished Mr. Jenkins was here. She banged again. Hurry, please hurry, she thought. Toby needs help . . .

The window in the room where Mr. Jenkins slept slid open and a sleepy voice called, "Who's there?"

It was Mr. Jenkins! Never had she been so glad to hear that familiar voice.

"Mr. Jenkins! Oh, Mr. Jenkins! You're back!" she cried.

"Anna? Good heavens, Anna! Is that you?"

She heard his footsteps racing towards her and in a minute he was at the door and she was in his arms, sobbing.

"Anna? What is it? Calm down now and try to tell me what's wrong."

"It's Toby," she managed to get out. "He's in the boat. He's half dead, I think."

Ben appeared behind Mr. Jenkins, rubbing his eyes sleepily. "What's going on, sir?"

Mr. Jenkins drew Anna into the lighthouse and sat her down. "Ben, get blankets, she's wet and half frozen. I'm going to get her brother."

Mr. Jenkins hurried across the deck, and Anna saw him disappear down the wooden walkway to the rocks.

In a minute Ben appeared with a pile of blankets. "Here. You must be frozen." He handed her the blankets and then said, "I'm going to help Mr. Jenkins," and ran out, leaving Anna to wrap herself in them.

She wanted to follow them, but all of a sudden she felt as if she couldn't move. She slumped back in the chair, cold and exhausted.

In minutes Mr. Jenkins and Ben came into the room carrying Toby. "Let's put him in my bed," Mr. Jenkins said, and they continued through the room to the door that led to the bunk room.

Mr. Jenkins came back into the sitting room and went to the woodstove. He opened it and began to stoke it. "Let's get some heat in here and get you unfrozen, and then I want to know how you came to be out in a dory, soaking wet, in the middle of the night," he told her. "Ben, put the kettle on and we'll give Anna some hot tea."

"I'm so glad you're back," Anna said. "I thought you'd still be up in Baltimore."

Mr. Jenkins nodded. "I had expected to stay until tomorrow, but what I found out up there made me decide I had better come home as quickly as I could."

"What do you mean?"

"I went to see a German friend of mine who helped me translate the letter. It made me realize that Toby was in grave danger. But what about you? What happened?"

"I . . . I kept getting feelings. You know how Toby and I are, how we communicate?"

Mr. Jenkins nodded. He had known them since they were babies, and he seemed to understand.

"I just knew that he was in trouble and I had to get him off that boat. I couldn't wait any longer."

"From the look of him it's a good thing you didn't," Mr. Jenkins said.

"Will he be all right?" Anna asked, tears filling her eyes again.

"I think so. He just needs rest right now," Mr. Jenkins said as Ben handed Anna a steaming cup of tea. "But as for his friend Otto, I'm afraid he wasn't so lucky."

Otto. Otto is dead. Anna had known that from the beginning.

"Otto wrote the letter, didn't he?" Anna asked.

"Yes," Mr. Jenkins nodded. "Otto was a German boy. He wrote the letter, and then when he knew he was about to die he gave it to Toby. Somehow Toby found a way to mail it to you."

"What does the letter say?" Anna asked.

"I have a rough translation that my friend gave me," Mr. Jenkins said. He went to the desk in the corner of the room, took out a folded piece of paper, and handed it to Anna.

Anna unfolded it and read:

To Whom It May Concern,

I, Otto Ferdinand Grüner, write this letter to testify to the grievous abuse and maltreatment which I and others have received at the hands of Captain Jake Neville and the certain members of the crew of the Eva.

I write these words with the last of my strength. I am sick and beaten unto death, and do not expect to survive this voyage. I pray that my words may prevent others from suffering a similar fate.

I entrust this letter to my friend and fellow sufferer Tobias Shipherd. I pray that he may escape this hell-hole with his life and that he lives to seek justice.

To God am I now committed. May His will be done.

Otto Ferdinand Grüner

As Anna read the letter she felt tears start in her eyes again. How sad it was. A young man, Toby's friend, dead.

"It's terrible, isn't it?" Mr. Jenkins said.

Anna nodded. "What will happen now?" she asked.

"We will use the letter to get Captain Neville brought to justice. Just as Otto intended," he said.

"Yes," said Anna. "Yes, that's what he wanted. That's why he wrote the letter." And suddenly it came to her. "And they knew. They knew about the letter. That's why he was spying on me."

"Who? Who was spying on you, Anna?" asked Mr. Jenkins.

"The man with the oyster hand. He was in Crick's the day it came in the mail. And then I saw him out in our yard one night. But Willy scared him off. And someone dug up my tin box in the old lighthouse. It must have been him, looking for the letter." She shivered as a vision of the man's cruel face swam before her eyes. "So they must have known about the letter. I wonder how Toby managed to mail it."

"We'll find out when Toby is recovered and able to explain it," Mr. Jenkins said gently. "But in the meantime, we'd better get you home."

Anna looked out across the water. A streak of dawn showed on the horizon. "My father's probably already left," she said. "He probably doesn't even know I'm gone."

"Will he be looking for the dory?" Mr. Jenkins asked.

Anna shook her head. "His boat is at the town dock in the harbor."

"Well, someone will soon notice that you're missing, if they haven't already. Your mother's got enough on her mind with Toby being gone. Let's get you home before she misses you."

"What about Toby?" Anna asked.

"I'm going to leave him here for now. Ben will stay with him. Later today we'll get Doc Hollis out here to look him over, and if he says it's okay, we'll move him back home. Until then, I expect the best thing for him is rest."

Anna nodded. "I just want to say goodbye," she said, going to the door that led to the bunk room.

Toby lay in Mr. Jenkins's bed, covered with quilts. His face was so pale, so thin. He looked as if he had grown older in the few weeks he had been gone.

"Toby?" Anna crept to the bed and whispered, "Toby?"

She put her hand to his cheek. "Toby?"

"Anna," his eyes flickered and opened. He looked at her without recognition, and then, "Anna? Where am I? What's happened?"

"You're at the lighthouse with Mr. Jenkins," Anna told him.

"The lighthouse? But what about Captain Neville? Will he come after me? I don't want to go back to that boat."

"No. No, Toby, you won't have to. You're safe here. Soon we'll take you home."

"Anna?" Tears were rolling down his cheeks.

"Shhh. You should sleep now."

"But Anna, Otto is dead."

"I know, Toby, I know. Toby, I have to go now, but I'll see you later."

"Anna?" He reached out and touched her hand.

"What, Toby?"

"I missed you."

"Come on, Anna, we need to get you home." Mr. Jenkins stood in the doorway to the bunk room.

She turned and followed Mr. Jenkins. It was sad that Otto was dead, but Toby was okay, and she, Anna, had saved him. All by herself, she had saved him.

Twelve

"Mama! Mama!" Anna ran across the parlor and into the kitchen.

Her mother turned from the stove with a gasp. "Good Lord, child, you startled me. What on earth . . .?"

"Oh, Mama." Suddenly Anna felt no older than Margaret. Tears were running down her cheeks again, and before she knew it she was in her mother's arms and sobbing.

"Anna, child, what is it? Where are your clothes?"

"Oh, Mama, Toby—"

"Toby?" Her mother took Anna's face in her hands and looked at her. "Did you find out where he is? Is he all right?"

"Yes, Mama, yes, he's all right, but—"

Mr. Jenkins spoke up behind Anna.

"He's all right, thanks to Anna here. That's quite a girl you've got, Emma Shipherd."

"I don't need you to tell me that, Mr. Jenkins. I'm well aware of that fact, thank you." She looked at Anna again. "Now, what about Toby?"

"He's at Mr. Jenkins's. In the lighthouse. He's, he's—" Anna looked at Mr. Jenkins. "He's okay, but . . ."

"He's going to need rest, and I want Doc Hollis to take a look at him. He's got a bad oyster hand, he's probably terribly malnourished, and I don't know what else. He'll be all right, Emma, but it will be a while before he's the hale and hearty boy you're used to seeing."

Her mother's eyes hardened. "Those drudgers. He should never have gone off with them. Evil. Evil men."

"Yes, well, thanks to Anna here, he'll be all right. I would say she saved his life."

Her mother hugged her again and said, "You're wet and cold, child. Come by the stove and tell me what happened."

Anna's mother wrapped her in a blanket and settled her into the rocker, pulling it up close to the woodstove. The heat from the fire and her mother's hovering presence swirled around Anna, wrapping her in a cloud of warmth and happiness. She was exhausted, but she felt good.

"So. Tell me. How did you come to be out half-dressed in the middle of the night? And how did your hair get wet?"

Anna told her about the notes, about the letter, and about seeing the man with the oyster hand.

"But why didn't you tell me any of this before, Anna?" her mother asked.

"I didn't think Toby wanted me to. I knew how angry Pa was, is, at him, and . . . I knew you were worried. I just didn't want to make it any worse."

"But what made you go out there in the middle of the night? How did you know what boat he was on?" Her mother's questions came faster than Anna could answer them, but she tried to explain it all as best she could. She knew that some of it was hard to understand, hard to explain, but her mother understood better than anyone else how she and Toby knew each other's thoughts. After all, she had raised them and had seen it firsthand.

When Anna got to the part about the man on the oyster boat grabbing her, her mother's eyes grew wide. "Oh Anna, you could have been killed. You should never have gone out there alone."

"But I had to, Mama," Anna told her.

"I know, but . . ."

"It's okay, Mama. We're both okay."

Two days later, Toby, looking much more like himself than he had when he came home, sat propped up on the couch near the woodstove in the parlor. He had insisted on moving out of the bedroom. "I want to be in the middle of things, Ma. It's boring back there," he said.

"You're recuperating. It's supposed to be boring," Anna told him.

"I'm already recuperated," Toby said.

Noah sat on the floor beside the couch with the broken muskrat trap. Toby was helping him repair it.

Gradually, over the past two days, Toby had told them the horrible story of his time on the oyster boat. He told them how Captain Neville had beaten and starved them, and how Otto, who had gotten sick shortly after boarding the ship, had finally died of starvation and physical abuse.

"Did he beat you every day?" Noah asked Toby, his eyes wide.

Toby nodded. "In the beginning he beat us all the time, even if we hadn't done anything wrong. He's mad. Even his own crew knew it. But once Otto died, they got worried. I think they knew it had gone too far," Toby said. "That's when they put me in the box and just kept me there. I don't know what they were planning," he added with a shudder. "I guess they were worried I'd try to escape, which I would have if I'd had the chance. Lucky I managed to sneak Otto's letter to a fellow on the buy boat to mail for me."

"So that's how you mailed it. I wondered," Anna said. She and Margaret were sitting on the floor in front of the woodstove. Anna was trying to teach Margaret to play cat's cradle.

Toby nodded. "But Captain Neville must have found out about the letter somehow, and realized it would prove that he murdered Otto. That's why he sent Gus Crowder after you. To try to get the letter."

"Gus Crowder? The man with the oyster hand?" Anna asked.

Toby nodded. The haunted look returned for a minute, and then was gone. "I wouldn't dignify him by calling him a man. Swine is more fittin'." Toby smiled. "I wish I'd been awake when you bashed him over the head. What a sight that must have been."

There was a knock on the door, and Margaret ran to answer it.

Mr. Grim stood in the doorway, dressed as usual in his city clothes, his hat in his hand. He bowed slightly to Margaret and said with a smile, "Good day, Miss Shipherd. I've come to inquire after the patient."

Anna stood up. "Mr. Grim! Come in. Just a minute and I'll get Mama."

Anna poked her head into the kitchen where her mother stood at the stove stirring a pot of fish stew. "Mama, Mr. Grim's here. He's come to call on Toby."

"How thoughtful of him." Her mother put the lid on the stew and followed Anna out of the kitchen.

"Mr. Grim. How kind of you to call," she said. "Won't you sit down?"

"Thank you, Mrs. Shipherd." Mr. Grim sat on the chair her mother indicated.

"This is Toby," Noah said, pointing proudly to his brother. "He almost died but Anna saved him."

"Thank you, Noah," Mr. Grim said, hiding a smile. He offered his hand to Toby. "Hello, son. I hear you've had quite an adventure."

"Yessir," Toby answered, shaking Mr. Grim's hand.

"From the look of him he's recovering nicely," Mr. Grim said to Anna's mother.

"Yes. He's doing very well, considering."

"Yes, considering," Mr. Grim said. He held his hat in his lap and fiddled with the brim. He seems nervous, Anna thought, and suddenly she remembered how he had been talking to Gus Crowder. Was he involved somehow with Captain Neville?

"Can I get you some tea, Mr. Grim?" her mother offered.

"No, thank you, ma'am." He paused, and then went on, "I . . . I'm here, actually, to discuss something with you all."

"Something about the children's schooling, sir?" her mother inquired.

"Not exactly, ma'am. You see, I must confess that I am not really a schoolteacher."

Anna gasped. So it was true. She and Nellie had known there was something odd about him. And now he was admitting it.

"Not a schoolteacher?" her mother said.

"No. I'm a reporter for the Baltimore *Sun* newspaper. When my friend Miss Winslow, who was hired to teach in your school, had to stay in Baltimore to care for her father, I volunteered to take her post temporarily. You see, my paper wanted me to do a story on the oyster industry. I wanted to find out all I could about the oystermen and coming to Heron's Harbor seemed a good way to do that."

"Will you still teach us?" Noah asked.

"Just for another week. Now that Miss Winslow's father is recovering, she will be coming to take up her post soon, and I will go back to Baltimore."

"A reporter!" Anna cried. "Is that why you were talking to Gus Crowder? I saw you down by the docks . . ."

"Yes. I saw that he had an oyster hand, and I asked him what boat he'd been on. He wasn't very helpful, however."

"Helpful," Toby snorted. "Gus Crowder wouldn't help a newborn baby, lest his name was Captain Neville."

"Yes, so I surmised. A singularly unpleasant man." Mr. Grim turned to Toby. "I was wondering, Toby, if you'd be willing to tell me about your, er, experiences? I'd like to include your information in my article."

Anna's mother spoke up. "I don't think he's up to . . ."

"Forgive me, ma'am," Mr. Grim said quickly. "I didn't mean now, of course. I know he's still recuperating and needs his rest, but perhaps when he's feeling better?"

"Sure," said Toby. "Will I be in the Baltimore paper?"

"Just a minute, Tobias," said Mrs. Shipherd. "The first thing we have to do is see that these men are brought to justice. After that we can talk about newspaper articles and such."

"Yes, ma'am," Mr. Grim agreed. "And I believe I may be able to help you with that. I have the names of some people in Baltimore." He took a list from his breast pocket.

Anna's mother took the list and studied it.

"What's this you have here, Noah?" Mr. Grim asked, looking at the muskrat trap, and within minutes he was kneeling beside Noah on the floor helping him repair the trap.

When they had finished, Mr. Grim said, "Well, I'd best take my leave. I don't want to tire the patient."

Anna's mother held out the list he had given her.

"Perhaps you could come back tomorrow night, Mr. Grim, when my husband is home, and we'll talk about all this."

"Of course, ma'am."

"Thank you for coming, Mr. Grim."

"Until tomorrow evening, ma'am."

Mr. Grim left and Anna and Margaret went back to their game of cat's cradle. Margaret picked up her string and tried to work it over her fingers. "Like this, Anna?" she asked.

"Here, wait," Anna took the string and stretched it over Margaret's fingers, and then took up her own string. "Now, like this, Margaret. Up, over, down."

From the kitchen came the smell of fish stew and corn bread.

And then, Anna heard her father's footsteps crossing the porch and in a minute he was inside, smelling of salt and oysters, his face ruddy with the cold and the weather.

He and Toby looked at each other. It was the first time they had really seen each other since Toby had come back. For the last two days, whenever her father had been home, Toby had been asleep, and her father had made no effort to see him.

Now he stood near the couch, his face stern and impassive. He said nothing. Will he forgive him, Anna wondered. Was he glad to see him? Her father was so hard to understand sometimes.

"You were right about the drudgers, Pa. I should'a listened to you," Toby said.

"You should have," Pa said. His voice was flat, emotionless.

"But Pa, all the money they make. And Captain Neville . . . He seemed so nice. He told me I'd come home rich."

"Hmmm," Pa grunted. "Lucky you come home at all. But for your sister here, you'd like to be crab bait by now."

"I know that, Pa. Yes, sir, I know that now. But I just had to try it. I had to see for myself. You know what I mean, Pa?"

There was a pause. The tension in the air was so thick it was hard to breathe. Then Pa's lip twitched the tiniest bit. He moved towards Toby and put a hand on his shoulder. "I reckon I know what you mean, boy. You're as stubborn as a blue crab, and twice as foolish."

"I know, Pa, but I learnt my lesson, I swear it."

"Until the next adventure comes along."

"No, sir. I watched a friend die. That's something I'll

never forget," Toby said sadly. He was quiet for a minute, and his eyes had a haunted look as if he were remembering something terrible.

Then he looked at Anna.

"Anna's the next one to have an adventure. When are you going to Baltimore?"

"How did you know . . . ?"

"It's all you've been thinking about lately. And I saw the letter you're writing to Aunt Phoebe."

Anna knew that Toby was right. She was going. She had to go. She looked around the cottage, full of the people and things that were nearest and dearest to her, and she knew how much she would miss them. But Toby was right, she had to go.

 *Thirteen*

Anna stood on the deck of the steamboat as it pulled away from the dock, away from Heron's Harbor. Her mother, Nellie, Margaret, and Noah stood below on the shore, waving. Noah was swinging both arms up and down in an arc, waving so hard that he fell right over, and Anna laughed. Now she was laughing and crying at the same time. I must look like a crazy person, she thought, taking out her handkerchief and wiping her eyes.

She was going to Baltimore to live with Aunt Phoebe and continue her schooling. She was leaving her home, and everything she had ever known. She was scared. What would it be like? Would the school be hard? Would she make new friends?

"I'll write you every day," Nellie had said when she hugged her goodbye, and maybe she would for a while, but Anna knew that, after a while, Nellie would forget to write.

Anna watched and waved until the steamer went around the bend, and she could no longer see the dock.

Then the lighthouse came into view, and Anna saw Mr. Jenkins on the deck, waving his cap.

They steamed past the shoals, and Anna scanned the water, looking for her father's boat.

There it was, and there they were, her father and Toby, standing side by side, watching for her as the boat steamed past.

Simultaneously, they each raised a hand, and Anna saw for the first time how much alike her father and Toby looked. She watched them until they were tiny specks on the greenish-brown water, and then, like the others on shore, they were gone, and she was all alone, crossing the Bay towards Baltimore.

Anna felt a momentary sense of panic as everything she had ever known passed from sight. But then, from somewhere inside her she heard Toby say, "Don't forget us, Anna."

And she knew, then, that they would always be with her, no matter how far she went, or how long she was gone.

Historical Note

Anna and her family lived on the Eastern Shore of the Chesapeake Bay in the 1880s. The Civil War had ended, but all over the Bay new battles, known today as the oyster wars, were taking place.

In the second half of the nineteenth century, three factors—new canning methods that allowed long-distance transport of oysters, the expansion of the railroads, and the booming postwar economy—had combined to cause an unprecedented growth in the oyster industry. Suddenly, everyone wanted oysters, and prices soared.

A get-rich-quick mentality invaded the sleepy Eastern Shore towns, and with it came corruption and lawlessness. In the late nineteenth century, there were five thousand oystermen on the Eastern Shore, and they were divided into two groups, the tongers and the dredgers (or "drudgers" as they were called).

The tongers, like Anna's father, used long-handled tongs to pull oysters up from shallow waters into a small boat. The drudgers worked in large sailboats pulling a metal scoop across the oyster beds in deeper waters. The tongers felt that the drudgers were destroying the beds, and saw the drudgers as evil men who were encroaching on their livelihood. Laws were established to protect the tongers' territory, but the drudgers were known for defying these laws.

Oysters were harvested in the coldest months of the year and the watermen had to withstand freezing water and cold winds. Tongers worked from sunup to sundown, returning home every evening, but the drudgers remained out on the Bay for weeks at a time. Tales of the hardships on board the dredge boats spread, and the dredge boat captains sometimes had a hard time finding crew members. Often, dredge boat captains, or their emissaries, would entice poor immigrants to sign on with promises of good working conditions and fair pay. But once on board these men became captive workers and were treated unmercifully. Many immigrants died or came near to death on the dredge boats.

Otto Grüner's character is based on the true story of Otto Mayher, a young German immigrant who died at the hands of Captain Williams of the dredge boat *Eva* in 1884.